***I SENSE EVIL
NOTHING MORE***

and yet there is a pall of dread that pervades the emptiness and follows me even here, aboard *Paulus*. As a member of the last generation of the Old Ones to be born on the home planet I have seen death, so it is not new to me. But I have come to think the destruction of Old Earth came not from deliberate malice, not from intent, but from ignorance. My planet was not killed instantly, as were the worlds of the sac. There is hope for Earth, but not for the Dead Worlds.

It is my feeling that there must have been savagery, barbarism, callous cruelty, something more than just an accidental slide into the ruining of worlds. Such total devastation had to be deliberate.

I cannot, at this moment, fully explain my feeling of melancholy empathy, my sense of dread. Perhaps I am confusing pure emotion with the data collected by my senses; but when I soared there on that airless world I felt something. Ghosts? A residual life force? Only time will tell. . . .

> —from the thoughts of Stella the Power Giver,
> day 3 of the Dead Worlds Expedition
> of LaConius of Tigian

THE
OMNIFICENCE
FACTOR

ZACH HUGHES

DAW BOOKS, INC.
DONALD A. WOLLHEIM, FOUNDER
375 Hudson Street, New York, NY 10014

ELIZABETH R. WOLLHEIM
SHEILA E. GILBERT
PUBLISHERS

Copyright © 1994 by Hugh Zachary.

All Rights Reserved.

Cover art by Martin Andrews.

DAW Book Collectors No. 939.

If you purchase this book without a cover you should be aware that this book may have been stolen property and reported as "unsold and destroyed" to the publisher. In such case neither the author nor the publisher has received any payment for this "stripped book."

First Printing, January 1994

1 2 3 4 5 6 7 8 9

DAW TRADEMARK REGISTERED
U.S. PAT. OFF. AND FOREIGN COUNTRIES
—MARCA REGISTRADA
HECHO EN U.S.A.

PRINTED IN THE U.S.A.

CHAPTER ONE

From the claustrophobic cockpit of an atmospheric scout the Tigian space yacht, *Paulus,* was a comforting sight. To the naked eye she was nothing more than a small, artificial dot reflecting the hard, harsh light of crowded millions of core stars. The scout's optics brought *Paulus* closer, showed her lines. She was built for space, her design ignoring traditional aesthetics in favor of maximum utility of the inboard areas. She was not beautiful, but it was reassuring to look at her now and then.

The scout's communicator came to life. "The light should be right soon, John." The speaker was LaConius of Tigian, young, the tone deceptively laid back, the words formed individually, slowly, with rich bass overtones. *Paulus* belonged to LaConius, or, more accurately, to his Tigian father. Surnames were recorded in the ship's log, but were seldom used by those aboard.

John had positioned the scout so that the yacht was in the upper right corner of the little vessel's recorder viewscreen. She would be a part of the composition when the light from the planet's sun struck the surface at just the right angle.

A world loomed above the tiny scout, rolling slowly

as it had for billions of years. John tested his equipment, made an exposure, played it back, and then erased it. He made one small adjustment and then there was nothing to do but wait. The recorder was programmed for continuous operation. He triggered it early because he didn't want to risk missing a moment of the proper combination of light and shadow on the planetary surface.

There were no obscuring clouds to concern him, because the planet had no atmosphere. The images on the screen were hard-edged and glaring as the area below the scout's stationary orbit edged into sunlight.

Suddenly the object of John's vigil began to emerge from the black of night. Cut into the barren rock of the airless world was a series of symbols designed to be of universal significance. The inscription consisted of two lines, one above the other, stretching for hundreds of miles across the sterile surface. The dark shadows cast low on the horizon by the planet's primary sun imparted a sinister feeling. John looked around uneasily and checked his detectors. He was alone. He printed test stills from the recorder, nodded in satisfaction. *Paulus* was a tiny, glowing star suspended in the blackness against the silver of the galactic core, a billion stars, a seething ocean of solar winds. Below *Paulus*, the planet filled the lower three quarters of the print. The inscription that had concerned the citizens of the United Planets for thousands of years was outlined dramatically in light and shadow.

John keyed the comkey, said, "Okay, I've got it."

"Come on home," LaConius said.

"I'm ready." He was more than ready. Being alone in the vastness of space made for a certain tenseness. On flux drive it would have taken him a full hour to run back to the *Paulus*. He had programmed a reciprocal course on the way out and was thus able to activate the blink drive to get back to the ship. There was no problem charging the generator so near galactic center. Even in the relatively uncrowded sac where *Paulus* lay, the generator's seeker could choose from dozens of solar power sources.

The scout blinked back into normal space within fifty feet of the yacht's air lock. John closed the distance quickly and skillfully. A click of metal indicated union. There was an audible hiss of air as pressure was equalized between the scout and the larger ship.

Cecile was at the lock controls. She was the laughing one. Her green eyes smiled with her lips. Her sunbright hair was short and fluffy. To see happy Cecile's face become serious, as it did when John handed her a copy of one of the better stills, was a rare experience. Even, white teeth gnawed at her lower lip for a moment before she glanced up.

"It's impressive, in a rather terrible way," she said.

John nodded. They walked together to the lounge where John displayed large prints on the bulletin board over the bar.

LaConius, dark, tall, his tightly curled hair a cap over his well-shaped skull, sprawled with one leg draped over the arm of his chair. His eyes were dark brown. His nose hawkish. Near him sat quiet Martha of Terra II, the home planet. Her primly crossed legs were encased in a body stocking that matched the color of her modest sheath. Her mouse-brown hair was shoulder length when she let it hang free, which was seldom. Her face was pleasantly regular. She was as attractive as Cecile in her own way, but less flamboyant about it. She was proud of being a native of old, sick Terra II, the planet of original settlement.

The other four members of the *Paulus* expedition were Old Earthers. Two of them were in the lounge. Stella, the Old Earth female, was clad only in her coat of tiny, multihued protective scales. In shape she was pleasingly humanoid. Her shielded eyes were a startling blue. Rainbow-tinted scales formed a thick, hairlike mass atop her delicate head.

Clear Thought, Healer, another member of the older division of the human race that had mutated into four distinct survival forms in the poisoned atmosphere of Old Earth, was even more thoroughly armored than Stella. He was powerfully built, somewhat bulky. His organically filtered breathing apparatus could find scattered atoms of oxygen in the most polluted air. His armor allowed him to endure radiation deadly to soft-skinned Homo Sapien Sapiens like LaConius, John, Cecile, and Martha.

"Nice work, John," LaConius said with his rich, slow accent. "It was worth the wait."

John felt the mind of One Alone, the Far Seer, another Old Earther, and perhaps the strangest. They had agreed to leave the rules of privacy behind them on Xanthos. For safety and for maximum effectiveness, One Alone was free to communicate mentally at any time. They were friends. They had worked together for a full standard year preparing for the expedition.

One Alone's message was not in words. John sensed praise for his work.

"What do you think, Martha?" John asked.

Martha nodded. "Impressive. Spooky." She smiled at

John and her face took on a tantalizing vitality. "It speaks out, doesn't it?"

"Yes," Cecile said. "It says, 'Hey, baby, wouldn't you rather be back at good old Xanthos U. doing a term paper in home economics?' "

"To me it says, 'I've got a secret,' " LaConius said. "It's not going to give up that secret easily, but there are answers here if we look hard enough and far enough."

"I'm not sure that I really want to know," Martha said softly.

"You should feel at home on a dead world after growing up on a used-up ball of mud like Terra II," LaConius said.

"There's breathable air on Terra II," Martha said.

"Of a sort," Cecile said.

"And there's life," Martha continued.

LaConius laughed. "Yes, a few stubborn dreamers and some crawly things."

"Actually," Stella said, "reclamation of the ecosystems on Terra II is quite well advanced."

LaConius was staring at the pictures that glowed in three dimensions. A silence fell over the group in the lounge. Cecile cleared her throat. It was Clear Thought who broke the silence.

"When?" he asked. There was no need to explain the question.

"Now," John said.

"Whee," Cecile said, twirling her finger in the air in feigned excitement.

"One Alone?" LaConius asked aloud.

They all heard, or felt, the Far Seer's mental message of acknowledgment.

"Want to hold the fort?" LaConius asked.

One Alone sent an affirmative answer.

"Let's go, while there's still sunlight," LaConius said. "One Alone, we'll probably stay on the surface through a night cycle. We'll sleep in the scouts, finish the survey tomorrow, and then move on."

Cecile said, "Cone, would you mind taking me home before you go down there? I think I hear my mother calling."

"Oh, sure," LaConius said. "Since it's only a few hundred parsecs."

"Take one of the scouts," John teased.

"I'd have to pack a lunch," Cecile said. "Too much trouble."

John gazed at the pictures, let the shadowed outlines of the inscription burn into his mind. He was large for a native of Selbelle III, standing a slim, well built six-three. He wore his dark hair long. His eyes were the eyes of an artist. He was the senior New Earther in age and he had not yet reached the mid-mark of his twenties.

Martha came to stand beside him. "Deep thoughts?"

"I was remembering Prof. Paulus' lectures on linguistics. This is one instance of interracial communication that doesn't fit his theories."

Martha nodded. "He felt that intelligence evolves rarely and in ways so different that it is almost impossible for two distinct and unrelated species to communicate."

"He had good reason to believe that, since the only alien language known was that discovered in the Miaree manuscripts," John said. "To be fair to him, this inscription could be called a sign language."

"It's all too easy to understand," Martha said.

"With the possible exception of that one symbol." John pointed. "The one that is usually taken to mean aspire."

"Or hope, or love, or some other abstract verb."

"Perhaps that sign was intended to be ambiguous," Clear Thought said, as he looked over their shoulders. "Perhaps they wanted it to mean different things to different people, to cover the goals or aims of any race that might come across it."

"Whatever they meant, they have my attention," Cecile said. "I keep wondering if they killed that world just to have a canvas on which to draw the warning."

John read the inscription in a low voice. "Look on this, you who aspire, and quake. Build not, for we shall return."

For long moments there was only the sound of ship's housekeeping mechanisms, the click of servos, the muttering of the life-support system, the unheard but felt hum of the blink generator.

Cecile closed her eyes and listened to the sounds that had become familiar, homey. When she opened her eyes, she turned to a viewscreen. All of space was on the screen, velvet blackness sparkled with the crowding core stars. She shivered as she thought of the storms of radiation that were being turned aside by the ship's deflectors.

"Coming, Cecile?" John asked.

"Why not?" she asked, tossing her bright hair.

CHAPTER TWO

Two trim and agile scouts rested on planetary bedrock with hatches joined. As the nightline moved past, the dark cold of space was abruptly replaced by the unfiltered, raw glare of the sun. The landing site was on a small rise a few hundred feet from the western end of the deeply carved inscription. LaConius was napping aboard the Number Two scout. The Old Earthers, Clear Thought the Healer and Stella the Power Giver, were recording and checking instrument readings and comparing their data with their own sensed observations.

The *Paulus* expedition was by no means the first to visit the Dead Worlds, so neither Clear Thought nor Stella anticipated finding anything new on the outermost of the sac worlds, which was called DW-1 on the star charts. One Alone the Seer said it was presumptuous to think that a group of graduate students would discover anything significantly new on any of the Dead Worlds.

The orbit of DW-1 lay across the approach lane to a close grouping of G class stars huddled together as if for reassurance in a space sac dwarfed by the oceans of old, huge, cruel central core monsters. The choice of

DW-I for the warning inscription was an obvious one, since any ship approaching the sector had to skirt around a dense cluster of blue giants that blocked a straight-line approach to the relatively roomy sac.

Planets of any sort were not common enough to be ignored. Any visitor coming close enough to detect the lesser body orbiting the first of the Dead Worlds stars would want to take a close look at DW-I and, thus, see the message carved so deeply into the planet's exposed bones. The most basic of analysis instruments would convince any visitor that the planet was, indeed, dead.

John, standing watch on the Number One scout, was considering the condition of DW-I, thinking how simple it is to kill a human being as contrasted with killing an entire world. Man is a soft, vulnerable, fragile thing to whom the universe shows pity in the form of a sparse scattering of water worlds suitable for human life. Man can be killed in a myriad of ways. On a grander scale, it is not all that difficult to denude a planet of forests. Man had done that on at least two worlds, Old Earth and Terra II. Animal species can be utilized or crowded into extinction. Atmosphere and oceans can be poisoned, but still, John was thinking, it's a neat trick to kill a planet as thoroughly and as completely as DW-I had been killed.

She'd been sterilized with a ruthless efficiency and a totality that belied the difficulty of the feat. A scan of the planet's surface was thought provoking. She was a world of barren rock, and although others in the sac were not quite as stark as DW-I, nowhere was there so much as a living unicellular or microscopic organism. Some being or beings, at some time in the past, had done a unique piece of work, for DW-I was cold to her core, a condition that contradicted several accepted rules of physics. The fact that an old and bulky planet had been killed so completely that her mass could no longer heat her core was just one of the unanswered questions that had kept United Planets astrophysicists making new guesses from the time of the first discovery of that group of planets that had come to be called the Dead Worlds.

That several of the worlds in the sac were dead from the inside out was one of the more frightening aspects of the Dead Worlds phenomenon. Unidentifiable rubble on some of the worlds, and the position of most of the planets in what should have been the life zone of their suns, indicated that once they had lived, had been blanketed with sweet air, liquid water oceans, and forests. Once the core of DW-I had been molten and there'd been volcanic activity. On other worlds, the pulverized rubble yielded tiny crumbs of refined metals and materials formed from artificial combinations of molecules. It was impossible to judge the exact stage of advancement, but it was certain that a technological civilization had existed on several of the sac worlds.

To reconcile such a past with a rocky surface having no top soil, no sandy products of past erosion, no water, no air, was difficult. To imagine what power had left DW-I with nothing more than her orbital motion and her axial rotation was impossible.

The members of the *Paulus* expedition, both the New Ones and the mutated Old Ones, could trace their origins back to Old Earth through a span of time that varied in the estimate, depending on the source. Since the reunion of the two branches of the human race, it had become fairly well accepted that man had been in space for something on the order of 30,000 years, with a relatively short hiatus following the first exodus from doomed Earth during which man pulled himself up from a new dark age and blasted his way back into space at the expense of the resources of a planet. Over the millennia, weapons had been developed, of course, for although man's origin and his early history were lost and were only now being studied in the archaeological digs in the poisoned soil of Old Earth, he had clung to the belief that there is good in the universe and there is evil, and it is the duty of good to stand in the way of evil.

So it was that there were weapons capable of shattering a world. To man's credit, or his shame, such planet-destroying weapons had been used only once, and then sparingly. Life zone planets were too rare, too valuable, to be made into asteroid belts, even if they were inhabited by men whom other men considered to be evil. Historical man, judging from the fragments being excavated on Old Earth, had been content with killing his fellows, leaving the air and water and the planet intact for his own use until things got out of hand at the end of the Nuclear Age. It was a testimony to man's adaptability that there were survivors of the final cataclysm. Those who had poisoned the Earth were the Old Ones, the ancestors of both the few who made the long and dangerous journey across space to Terra II, and those who mutated into that race of New Ones in their four symbiotic forms.

True, man could be deadly. True, he could smash a planet, bursting it at the core to send molten material spewing into cold space to harden and join other fragments in an eternal dance of death in what had been the orbit of a living world, but to date no one had come up with a weapon that would cool the core of a Terra II sized planet such as DW-I. It was difficult enough to imagine how the initial cooling could be accomplished. It was headache-producing to try to devise a scientific scenario that would keep the core of a world cold for thousands of years. The best estimates said that the planets of the Dead Worlds systems had been destroyed approximately 75,000 New Years in the past.

Small wonder, then, John was thinking, that the sac worlds haunted humanity. From the time of the discovery of the Dead Worlds the sac system had exerted a heavy influence on the thinking of the race. Because of DW-I and her sister worlds, the ships of the Department of Exploration and Alien Search carried armaments powerful enough to blast a world. Because of DW-I and the inscription carved into her surface the U.P. Council was always willing to allocate funds for the development of ever more terrible weapons, although the last known conflict in history, the Zede War, was ancient history.

Weapons were developed. Weapons were manufactured. Weapons were mounted on X&A's ships because one day, without warning, the destroyers might come sweeping in from interstellar or intergalactic space on wings of fire and unknown force. They had warned that such would happen.

"Look on this, you who aspire, and quake. Build not, for we shall return."

It was estimated that two hundred billion people had lived, and died, on the twenty Dead Worlds. For thousands of years, ships had come in from the U.P. worlds near the periphery of the galaxy to catalog and study that score of planets. After thousands of years, the answers were still elusive.

John had made light pictures during the glare of day. He was sorting them when LaConius, roused from his nap for the evening meal, carried his food tray into Number Two and studied the pictures while balancing the tray on his knee.

"If you were going to paint a representative view of DW-I, how would you start?" LaConius asked idly.

"I'd put bloods and blacks on my palette," John said.

Martha came in with a clipboard in her hand. "No change in readings since the last expedition was here," she said.

"Only living things change," Clear Thought said.

"Don't be so philosophical, Lizard Face," LaConius said.

Clear Thought, with his armorlike skin, ignored the gibe. His scaled face was incapable of the flexibility of an outward smile. "You're letting my masculine beauty eat at you," he said. Unlike many of their softer cousins, Old Earthers did not suffer self-image problems. As individuals, Healers and Power Givers were physically superior to the New Ones. As a working unit, a cadre of Old Earthers composed of Healer, Power Giver, Seer, and the Seer's idiot savant, the very human-looking Keeper, formed an intellectual unit that was prized throughout the U.P. All X&A exploration ships had their Old Earthers, and, to the chagrin of many, Seers especially were earning promotion to fleet rank in numbers.

"We haven't had a report from you, Stella," John said.

Stella had been silent since the scouts had landed on the planetary surface. She smiled at John. Her tiny, multicolored scales glistened, giving her an appearance of delicate femininity.

"Do things feel right to you?" John asked.

"Yes, with reservations," Stella said. "I can sense the planet's magnetic field. It's there, and I could soar on it, but—"

"But?" Martha asked.

"There's a difference that I can't explain."

"Perhaps," said One Alone from his cabin aboard *Paulus*, "the magnetic field is affected by the lack of heat at the core." He spoke only to Stella. "When you are ready, please record your first impressions."

"Now, if it's convenient," Stella said. She closed her eyes and felt the soft-warm contact of One Alone's Keeper. She recorded her findings.

Stella knew as well as anyone that she and the other Old Earthers were the prime reason why Council had permitted still another expedition to the Dead Worlds. For the first time since reunification of the two branches of the race the specific abilities of the mutants would be applied to the age-old enigma.

"Are you back with us, Stella?" John asked.

"Just recording to the Keeper," she said.

"If anyone is interested, he can record some ladylike snores from my bunk in short order," Cecile said. She smiled at LaConius. "Unless Cone wants to reconsider and go back to the ship."

"Go to bed," LaConius said.

In her berth Cecile felt sleep coming on quickly. Her last waking thoughts concerned the Old Earthers. How nice it would be, she mused, to have One Alone's mental telepathy, and Stella's ability to utilize the magnetic field of a planet to fly, or even Clear Thought's protection against radiation. She pulled the covers up tightly around her ears, because only a thin, single plate bulkhead separated her from the vacuum of space.

Nothing moved. There was, of course, no sound. The blackness of space pushed down to the surface, engulfing the two small craft joined at the middle. The stars were hard, too bright, weightily threatening in their density.

The rise of DW-I's primary sun brought instant, broiling day. Martha volunteered to stand shipboard watch. The other members of the ground party left the scouts as a unit. They wore the latest in life-support gear. John led the way across the scorched, barren rock to the edge of a sheer precipice which marked the beginning of the first sign of the inscription. The sides of the cut into sheer rock were glassy smooth.

"A disassembler could do this," LaConius said.

"Except for the fusing of the rock, mining instruments could do it," Cecile said.

Each individual element of the inscription had dimensions measured in the hundreds of miles. Stella soared high, riding the magnetic field of the planet, to get an aerial view. From two thousand feet she saw the deep cuts perspecting away toward the curve of the horizon. Her friends were reduced to shining dots on the ground as their space armor reflected the harsh sunlight.

There was nothing to be gained by spending more time on DW-I. Many expeditions with more complicated equipment and with more members had swept over the stark rock of DW-I in the past. Just for the record, they took a few rock samples. As the scouts soared, flux drives humming, they watched the inscription come entirely into their field of view as their altitude increased. It was a subdued group of explorers who shed their armor in the inner lock aboard *Paulus*.

CHAPTER THREE

These are the thoughts of Stella the Power Giver delivered into the mind of Soft Star, the Keeper of One Alone the Far Seer, on Day 3 of the Dead Worlds Expedition of LaConius of Tigian:

I sense evil here. Nothing moves. Nothing lives, and yet there is a pall of dread that pervades the emptiness and follows me even here, aboard Paulus. As a member of the last generation of the Old Ones to be born on the home planet I have seen death, so it is not new to me. As a child I saw my dear, old Earth struggle to stay alive. I was there when the microorganisms of the ocean, the Breathers who replenished the oxygen in the atmosphere, could no longer live and reproduce in the acid waters. As a child I soared in the poisoned atmosphere of my home world; and along with my race I waited for death.

I have come to think that the destruction of Old Earth came not from deliberate malice, not from intent, but from ignorance. My home planet was made unfit for the continued existence of the Old Ones, the original form of the human race, by the stupidity of a few men, not the entire race. Wars were planned and begun by an obtuse and egocentric minority, by a few political leaders. My planet was not killed instantly, as were the worlds in the sac. Moreover, since the reunification of the race, which came about because of the idealism of one man, Rack the Healer, vast sums of money are being spent to regenerate Earth's atmosphere and to cleanse her waters. There is hope for Earth, but not for DW-I.

It is my feeling that more than ignorance was in play here in this relatively uncrowded sac so near the deadly radiation storms of the galactic core. There must have been savagery, barbarism, callous cruelty, something more than just an almost accidental slide into the ruining of worlds. Such total devastation had to be deliberate.

We have a way of fouling our nests, we humans. Take Martha's planet, Terra II. It was simply used up. As the first planet to be settled by those who managed to escape Old Earth before the destruction, it was raped of its raw materials in man's eagerness to redevelop the technology to get back into space. What happened to Terra II is understandable. The race was relatively young. In the landing disaster, they had lost all records of their past, with the exception of one ancient book of religion. During the Age of Primitivism efforts were made to keep the history of the race, but not even scientists who had constructed a space-going vessel could record their complicated technical knowledge when there was no electronic or mechanical method of storing data. Oral tradition is limited to basic and simple ideas, to tales about gods and heroes. By the time there was paper to write on, long before the first simple computer was built, man had forgotten his planet of origin. Earth was lost among the stars, and to fulfill the longing of a race to find its home a planet was despoiled.

The race of man is not innocent. There are the radiation sumps on Earth to prove that. Once man used planet-destroying weapons against his fellows, but terrible *as that war was, civilization survived. The worlds of the defeated Zede system flower today. Only a few were destroyed.*

Planets suitable for human habitation are not plentiful. A living planet is a wondrously complicated mechanism, a cosmic rarity requiring a combination of qualities against which there are astronomical odds. The factors that go into finding water in liquid form on a planet are incredibly rare, and when the odds against conditions favorable to the creation of life are calculated we should consider a life zone planet to be a major miracle.

I shudder at the terrible waste that is so horribly illustrated by twenty dead worlds. Although I am curious and will do my part in exploration and study, I dread landing on the other worlds in the sac. I wonder what I will feel when I see further evidence of an unimaginable cataclysm.

It's difficult to accept the total inertness of DW-I. I keep comparing this world to Old Earth. Even after the wholesale use of nuclear weapons, some life endured and lasted for aeons in its losing fight against man's past stupidity. Even in the end, there was life. The atmosphere deteriorated to the point that it would not support the modest requirements of a Healer such as Clear Thought, but there were mutated life-forms, mostly in the form of rancid vegetation. But here? There is not even microscopic life.

I wonder how long it took to kill a score of worlds. An hour? A day? And what did they look like, these beings who had so little regard for life, the rarest and most sacred thing in the universe? I, who carry the genes of a race that had to fight to cling to life, cannot comprehend such evil. The power which carried Beautiful Wings the Power

Giver and her Rack on that flight which brought us into contact with the space-goers flows in me. From my birth I was taught to revere life, to cling to it when death was inevitable, to fight against the darkness not only for myself but for every living thing.

I wonder how they felt, the creatures of this dead world, when they knew that death was coming. Did they pray? Did they fight each other in desperation? Did they expect a last-minute miracle? On Old Earth, when all measurements said that there was no hope, we hoped, and there was a miracle of sorts. If these people hoped, they hoped in vain.

I cannot, at this moment, fully explain my feeling of melancholy empathy, my sense of dread. I don't know why there should be any visceral reaction on my part. Perhaps I am confusing pure emotion with the data collected by my senses; but when I soared there on that airless world I felt something. Ghosts? A residual life force? I know that such speculation is farfetched, and that it is most probably based on my emotions of horror and disbelief. I am traumatized to think of such mass extermination, so my dread is probably nothing more than a symptom of emotional pain, of the disquietude of being faced with cold, dead evidence of an inconceivable reality.

In the Book of Rack The Healer, it is stated: "We cannot conceive of malice until that malice is inflicted upon us."

When I was young I did not understand, nor did the people of Old Earth. Malice of any magnitude was an abstraction to us. We knew that Rose the Healer spoke enigmatically of hate as the cause of the destruction. Rose saw the terminal agonies of the old race in the time of troubles, but we, who came later, we who were so few, we to *whom one life was a treasure, did not comprehend. Rose the Healer, who witnessed the death of billions, might have been able to understand this world, and the nineteen others that orbit the sac suns. I confess that I cannot.*

CHAPTER FOUR

Log of the *Paulus*
Month 1, Day 3
Sector F-10 Tri-Chart Ref. F-10-1
Subject: Personal observations of DW-I, Sixth Planet,
Dead Worlds Primary Alpha
Signed: LaConius of Tigian

The U.P. Exploration Yacht *Paulus* orbiting DW-I.
Scout vehicles One and Two engaged in superficial
planetside survey. Landing local sunset, Month 1, Day
2. Lift-off shortly after local sunrise Day 3.

Observations of the research teams recorded main
computer. Observations show no change from last observations by Capt. Jackson G. Sparks, X&A Expedition
Ref. 225-558-1855-Z-323 *Official Records*. (See attached observation records.)

Personal remarks: She is very, very dead. It's a peculiar feeling to be down there. Surface temperatures
fluctuate as expected on an airless planet. What was
not expected, at least by me, was a feeling of coldness that had nothing to do with the temperature inside the scout or the life-support system of the armor
when we were surface-side. It was almost as if the

cold at the planet's core was seeping up into my bones.

I can understand why these worlds have boggled the finest scientific minds for thousands of years. Where is the force of compression at the core of this ball of rock? What in hell has happened in this one particular locality to the laws of mass? To find that an asteroid in open space has uniformly cold temperatures at its core would be no surprise, but in a planet the size of DW-I? No way.

The surface trip was uneventful. We wanted a close up look at the inscription and we had it. Nothing exciting. When you've seen one death warning from a departed killer race with the ability to cool the core of a planet and keep it that way forever, you've seen them all.

Cecile shows signs of nervousness. Aside from the Old Earthers she's the most sensitive one of us, apparently. Or is it that the others, including myself, are not willing to admit that they are affected? We're a long way from home with only those hard, hot, huge core suns around us and so close together that you couldn't blink a light-year without ripping the coils out of the generator. Maybe it's just all the hard stuff being puked out by those old core monsters that's affecting us in spite of shields and armor. Maybe it's just imagination. But there were some bad dudes around here at some time in the past. I find myself remembering all the space operas I've seen about the planet killers sweeping in from the big empty of intergalactic space with all guns firing. I dreamed about that last night and woke up in a cold sweat.

Nothing much new from the Old Earthers. Stella

says that the magnetic field of DW-I doesn't feel exactly right, but she can't come up with anything specifically different about it. I am still optimistic. I think we have a genuine opportunity here. With the help of Clear Thought, Stella, One Alone and that odd Keeper of his, I think we'll come up with some new data. I fully intend to go back to Xanthos and Tigian with something more than just another set of physical measurements.

Speaking of measurements reminds me of Paulus, he for whom this ship is named, and that damned literature-cum-philosophy-cum-humanities class of his. He said that man is the inchworm of the universe, always measuring. Well, not me. I'm not here just to reconfirm that there are twenty dead planets orbiting several pretty ordinary little suns in a hole in space near the core. I don't care if the instruments are not even unpacked. What I want is to record the sensations and reactions of the living instruments aboard, the Old Earthers. I'll be the first ever to make such a study here. I've got tools that no one has had before me. Stella flies under her own power and has marvelous intuitive reasoning fed by senses that are more acute—or something—than those of the "old" branch of the race. Clear Thought can live for an extended period of time in a hard vacuum and withstand the solar winds of a naked star. One Alone has sensory powers that defy any instrument ever constructed. He sees more without eyes than a United Planets observatory does.

No computer matches the versatility of a normal human brain, much less a brain like that of a Far Seer. When you add the storage capacity of the brain of that gooing, adult infant of a Keeper, when you add in the power of the ship's computer and combine everything with ordinary human intuition and reason, look out. We're going to come up with some answers or, at worst, with some interesting new questions.

It seems to me that a lot of meaningful advances in knowledge have come about simply because someone was in the right place at the right time. For example, Bradley Gore is famous because he had his X&A ship in the right sector of space, purely by accident, when Rack the Healer got the bright idea of using the soaring abilities of a Power Giver to go to the Earth's moon. Gore didn't do a damned thing except be there, and he's in the history books.

Well, I think I'm in the right place at the right time with the right tools. Move over Bradley Gore and you other old-timers. More over and make room in the history books for LaConius of Tigian. You're gonna hear from me.

Special Instructions: Restrict recall of Personal Remarks to LaConius of Tigian or, in the event of his death, to His Honor, John Iboni, President of the Federation of Tigian Planets.

CHAPTER FIVE

In the lounge Martha walked to the rectangular viewport and pushed the button that closed it. On the trip from Xanthos she had enjoyed the images of space, velvet blacks with a sprinkling of points of light against the backdrop of the Milky Way; but even something as beautiful as a star can become overwhelming in numbers. *Paulus* was a small, lonely ship circled about by brooding, ancient, glaring sources of hard radiation.

Like Old Earth, Terra II was located in a sparsely starred sector of the galaxy's rim. With Terra II as a starting point, the United Planets Confederation had developed in similar stellar neighborhoods, where there was breathing room, where a blinking ship could make jumps measured in multiple parsecs. From a planet in the U.P. system one could look up into a black sky at night to the pearl-white glow of the Milky Way without feeling as if the sky were about to fall.

"It is simply too heavy," Cecile had said, on first viewing the crowded millions of central core giants.

Heavy. The galaxy loomed over them in a burning, glowing mass. Even inside the relatively empty sector containing the Dead Worlds and their suns there was a feeling of being crowded. It was easy to turn one's thoughts further inward to that unknown point where a ship would be drawn into that furious, mysterious blackness which was the galaxy's heart.

No one objected to Martha's having closed the viewscreen. The lounge chairs were comfortable, the lights were low. Artificial gravity was set at three-quarters Xanthos normal. There was soft music, John's selections, and a feeling almost as if one were surface-side on a civilized planet in a small but luxurious apartment. Before being outfitted for the Dead Worlds expedition, the *Paulus* had been the number two personal yacht of the senior LaConius Iboni. Next to Zede-built ships, Tigian yachts were noted for their comfort, luxury, and dependability.

Cecile served refreshments. She had changed into a clinging silk one-piece leisure suit called a relaxer. She served herself and LaConius a Tigian mint mixer, to which she had been introduced by LaConius, himself. John was having Selbellese sherry while he scribbled on a pad with an antique pen. Martha was fighting a losing battle against Clear Thought in a word game.

Clear Thought scored with a ten letter word for a marine mammal of Xanthos.

"That's not fair," Martha said. "It isn't even your language."

Stella had wrapped her iridescent scales in sheer folds of silk. She sipped a fruit nectar while she was in silent communication with One Alone.

"I have read the near stars and the planet," One Alone said. "There is no information of note to be recorded."

"We didn't expect much of DW-1," Stella said.

"I have to admit, Cone," Cecile said, smiling over the top of her glass, "that you Tigians know how to live."

"All Tigians?" Martha asked, "Or just those whose father happens to be one of the richest men in the U.P.?"

"My father would be insulted by that remark," LaConius said.

"Sorry," Martha said, not too sincerely.

"My father would say he is the richest man in C Sector, and quite possibly in the whole U.P.," LaConius said.

"I believe," Cecile said. She poured a refill for LaConius and sat on the couch near him. "You know, Cone, when you first invited me to come on this trip I thought that it was just a new come-on you'd dreamed up."

"I never jive," LaConius said.

"I believed him immediately," John said. "I had seen him throw money around before." He grinned at Martha. "He's not the least bit ashamed of having more money than is really decent."

"Ashamed?" LaConius asked. "I could counter that in several ways. I could brush you off by saying that the poor are always with us and I don't choose to be one of them. If you were serious in your attack, and not just talking to hear your head rattle, I could put up a potent defense and point out to you that my family is wealthy because money is nothing more than a measure of service to others. I might even point out that the Iboni family has helped give the Tigian worlds the highest average standard of living in the U.P."

"Hey, I'm not complaining," Cecile said. "It's just that for the cost of this expedition you could have set up a rehabilitation center for the aged, or something lasting like that."

"The pursuit of knowledge is the most worthy of all causes," LaConius said.

"Need and plenty are the right and left hands of nature," Clear Thought said. "One of the things that amazed us most after the reunification was the fact that there are people who do not take advantage of universal free education, who—with jobs going begging in all fields—simply do not choose to work for themselves."

"Clear Thought is right," John said. "I don't think any of us have to apologize. Pure research is never a waste. Mankind makes advances based on new knowledge."

"Mankind advances on the backs of a few individuals," LaConius said.

"This is my night to be cynical," Cecile said. "Are we here in pursuit of knowledge or are we here to qualify in a rather interesting way for an advanced degree which will enhance our earning power in the flesh marketplace?"

LaConius yawned. "I am steeped in scholarly dedication to pure knowledge."

"He's searching, searching, searching," Cecile said.

"I have a definite goal," LaConius said.

"What are you searching for, Cone?" John asked.

LaConius shrugged. "Somewhere beyond space and time is wetter water, slimier slime." He smiled. "In case you don't recognize that line, it's from antiquity, thought to have been brought out from Old Earth by the first settlers. Recognize it, Lizard Face?"

"Not one of our writers," Clear Thought said. He was by nature a loner, but he liked the affectionate kidding he took from the Old Ones. He did not have the thought-reading ability of One Alone, but he was sensitive enough to what went on inside the skull of an Old One to know that when LaConius called him Lizard Face he was speaking with a certain sense of fondness.

"Wrong place for slime," Martha said. "At least not on DW-I."

"Sparks found water on DW-19," John said. "Water makes slime."

"Not the best slime," said LaConius.

"No slime, not even on DW-19," Stella said. "Slime is life."

"I wish we had mounted a deep drill rig," LaConius said. "It might be interesting to drill down a few thousand feet."

"If you had put any more equipment on board we wouldn't have room to breathe," Cecile said.

John was programming music. Knowing Cecile's taste for lively sounds he choose the running rhythm of a new wave of music from the outworld, Krans.

"Oh, yeah," Cecile said, leaping to her feet and extending her hand to LaConius.

"I'm bushed," LaConius said.

"You're always bushed," she said. She moved to stand in front of Clear Thought. "How about you, handsome? Dance with a poor, lonely, spurned girl?"

Clear Thought said, "Smile," which was his way of letting the Old Ones know that he was amused or pleased. His armored face did not show expression. His large chest was exposed, showing the armored scales that covered his body.

"Up and at 'em," Cecile said.

"My abilities do not include dancing," Clear Thought said. "Thank you for the invitation."

Cecile put the back of one hand to her forehead and looked languid. "Now I am really beginning to feel rejected," she said, turning to John.

"Dancing is frivolous," John said, winking at LaConius.

"Not to me," Cecile said, swaying to the music.

"Cecile, you have entirely too much feminine equipment to be flaunting it that way," LaConius said.

"What? What?" she demanded. "I'm just dancing."

"The way you do it is immoral," LaConius said.

Cecile did a bump and grind. "Suffer," she whispered, turning away to a corner to dance spiritedly by herself. When the music ended she fell into a chair, legs sprawled apart. "I could be with that group of real live wires who were going to do a dig on Old Earth," she said.

"Everyone's digging on Old Earth," LaConius said.

"I've never seen it," Cecile said. "Have you, Clear Thought?"

"I was quite young at the time of the removal," Clear Thought said. "I went back once. No man of my—no Healer is content until he has tested himself with the atmosphere of the home planet."

"Tell us about it," Cecile said.

"One Alone would have more accurate memories," Clear Thought said.

"If I may." One Alone's voice came into their minds. "All of you have seen the personal possessions of Rack the Healer in the Old Earth Museum on Xanthos. To him they were true treasure. He had his clothing, which was made of material fabricated from the com-

bined excretions of a spiderlike insect called a webber
and an antlike insect called a juicer. As you will agree,
his clothing would be scorned as the rags of the poor
on any U.P. world. He had a few small, corroded nug-
gets of metal, mostly aluminum and a form of steel. He
had a small supply of breathers, half-plant, half-animal.
Rack's possessions are symbolic of our life on Earth. By
far our most valuable possessions were air, water, food."

Now One Alone spoke in mind pictures. He showed
a small, isolated planet shrouded in deadly gases. He
showed soupy seas into which most of the planet's topsoil had eroded. Nothing lived in the seas except one
variety of seaweed, which was the principal source of
food, and the buglike breathers, who inhaled poison air
and exuded pure oxygen. He showed pictures of the
last days, when the four mutated forms of man gasped
for the last traces of oxygen in the dying atmosphere.
He gave them the taste of the food made from the one
surviving sea plant. He showed them nightmarish and
poisonous vegetation growing in the wet, low areas
where the soil was steeped in deadly radiation. He
showed them areas of barren rock and sterile sand.

For the first time in the many story sessions since the
trip began, he let them feel the true despair of the Far
Seers of Old Earth when it became certain that the race's
tenuous hold on life was to be broken as the breathers of
the ocean died. They knew the story of Rack the Healer,
called the New One, who had mutated to be able to extend his healing power into the bodies of others. He had
used his power to aid the soaring of his mate, Beautiful
Wings the Power Giver.

One Alone finished the session with mind pictures
of the long flight from Old Earth to the Moon, of the

death of both Rack and his Beautiful Wings, and of the coming of the X&A Exploration ship captained by Bradley J. Gore.

"He died thinking that he had failed," One Alone said. "But had he not made that incredible trip in search of a new place for habitation, I would be dead. All of us who lived on Old Earth would be dead."

"We ruined Earth and then we went into space and did it all over again, in a different way, on Terra II," Martha said moodily.

"Be a little forgiving," John said. "The settlers on Terra II had a racial memory of traveling in space. They did what they had to do to get back out among the stars. You can't really blame them for being in a hurry, if you can call taking 30,000 years hasty."

"Well, there is this," Martha said. "Not many people want to live on Terra II the way it is. So I own a city."

"A rat's nest of a city that is not good for much except archaeological digs," LaConius said.

"Still, it is my rat's nest," Martha said. "And remember this. Of the few thousand people who live on Terra II, there's probably a higher percentage of achievers than on any other planet. One of my neighbors is Mathais, the composer. John was playing his *Hymn to Miaree* just the other day. He says that the solitude of Terra II is good for his work."

"And on bad days he has to wear a breather when he goes outside," LaConius said.

"He rarely goes outside," Martha said. "He has adapted an entire complex of buildings to his needs. He couldn't afford to do that on any other planet. At my family home my dad has reconditioned an old observatory. We used to sit up there on the mountain top and study the stars. And there's nothing like atmospheric pollution for sunsets. You can't match our sunsets, anywhere."

"I like Xanthos, myself," Cecile said. "I like being with people, the more the merrier. I like to be able to see the latest plays and the newest experience films. I like going to galleries to see, for example, the latest exhibit from the artists of John's world, Selbelle III. All of you came from other worlds to attend the university. I was five minutes away by flier."

"The availability of various life-styles is one of the reasons for our scientific and artistic advances over the past few thousand years," John said. "If a man has ambition there are new worlds to conquer. There's always the challenge of a new frontier, always the opportunity to pit ourselves against nature, and the unknown. Old Paulus said that our continued expansion accounted for the fact that war has become a thing of the past."

"Maybe war isn't used as an instrument of political policy in modern times because we've become mature," Cecile said.

"I've just read Klong's *Theoretical History of Old Earth*," Clear Thought said. "He says that war served a useful purpose on Earth."

"Nonsense," Martha said.

"It's an alien concept to me, too," Clear Thought said, "but Klong believes that war was necessary to produce the technology required to get into space and to hold down a planet-locked population that threatened to halt all advances in favor of subsistence. That last concept is difficult for me. As you know, we Healers breed only once in a lifetime. Nature kept a balance among our four types. Each birth was a cause for celebration."

"But your Rose the Healer said that the Old Ones died in their billions," Cecile said. "Was that nature's way of keeping the balance?"

"Perhaps nature provides, but there are accidents," Clear Thought said.

"I believe in God," Martha said. "That's it, period."

"Perhaps we worship the same God," Clear Thought said. "By another name. We called him Nature."

"Evidentially the people who lived on DW-I didn't know Him," LaConius said.

"You can't say that with any certainty," Martha said. "The Artounee, Miaree's race, were monotheistic."

"And the Delanians?" LaConius asked.

"A killer race," Martha said. "Totally self-centered, willing to destroy a gentle people like the Artounee on the slight chance of saving themselves. But three out of four ain't bad. Both branches of humanity and the Artounee believed in One God. Three out of four."

"My guess is that the people who left twenty worlds dead were the champion atheists of all time," LaConius said. He got to his feet and stretched. "But we're not going to find all the answers here in the lounge. I'm off to bed."

"A worthwhile suggestion from a true leader of men," Clear Thought said.

"What did you write?" Martha asked.

"It's crude as yet," John said.

"I didn't think a Selbellian could write crudely. Let me see it."

"You can't read my writing," he said.

"Read it aloud, then."

"Please do," said LaConius, who was standing in the doorway.

"I was thinking of the Dead Worlds, and of Old Earth, and war. I was trying to understand how the people of Earth felt when they saw the clouds rise from the first salvo of bombs."

"Go on," Martha coaxed.

John lowered his eyes and kept them on the paper without looking up. "Ease peace. Eyes pose up! Dictate tranquil do thing true self. Soul sears not, belays beta burns. When Earth is torn, thunder fills the day and ash covers the night. Dose it, then. Club it. Tranquilize it. Try an antispasmodic, but where? Nerves don't break. Nerves char and melt and pain deeply in death. Ease peace, friend, and count blessings as you die. That rumble's not real. It's only testing, testing, testing, one, two. Call it planetary colonitis and remember, a smile's the best defense against fire storms, and ulcers don't sprout laughing."

Cecile made a face. "You're a little ray of sunshine."

"There is a certain sense of irony there," Clear Thought said.

"I am intrigued by the imagery," Stella said.

LaConius was unwilling to admit that he had felt a cold shiver up and down his back. "Well, this isn't lit class at the university. Let's call it a day."

"I'm with you," John said.

LaConius halted in the door again. "We're all acting as if these worlds have not been dead for 75,000 years. Let's remember that they are dead, and there's no mention of ghosts anywhere in a very copious record of explorations. The people who did the dirty work are as dead as the planets. They're not coming back. People have been coming into the sac for a few thousand years and no one has been eaten yet. If there were a threat here, it would have been discovered centuries ago."

"We hear, glorious leader," Cecile said, bowing.

"So let's knock off the paranoia. We're not here to get sentimental about people who have been dead for one helluva long time. We're here to find something, even if it's just one tiny new piece of information to shed new light on an old puzzle. I don't care if it's as simple as finding a push button to prove that the people of the Dead Worlds had fingers to use to blow themselves up. I just want this expedition to make some contribution."

"We hear, stalwart leader," Cecile said.

"All of us want that advanced degree. I want it as badly as any of you, perhaps more. I'll be standing for office in a few years and no man has ever been elected to high office on a Tigian planet without a terminal degree in one of the sciences. If you want to think that's the main reason why I'm here, that's Okay. You know that I wasn't the keenest scholar at Xanthos, and that my chances of earning a terminal degree in some field of theory were not all that good. Here I can earn it through action, and sheer plodding."

"You'll make a fine Chairman someday, Cone," John said.

"Don't worry, Cone," Cecile said. "We'll see that you get your degree." She moved to his side and took his arm. "And I agree with John that you'll make a good Planetary Chairman. You'll be my kind of public official. You'll leave well enough alone because you'll sleep through your entire term in office."

LaConius smiled down at her. "I have always maintained that the best thing that can happen in government is a decade-long holiday for all legislative bodies every eleven years." He was still talking when they reached the door to Cecile's cabin. "We've made enough laws to last for the next five thousand years."

"I might move to a Tigian planet just so I can vote for you, Cone," Cecile said. She stood on tiptoe and kissed him on the cheek. " 'Night."

"Your vote of confidence overwhelms me," LaConius said, reaching for her. She danced out of his grasp and closed the door behind her.

CHAPTER SIX

Log of *Paulus*
Month 1, Day 29
Sector F-10 Tri-Chart Ref. F-10-1
Position R-10, V-21.74, H-3.34, L-35.81
Subject: Second Planet of Star DW-H
Signed: LaConius of Tigian

U.P. Yacht *Paulus* holding orbit above Dead World 19. Arrival Month 1, Day 28 following flyby of Dead World planets 4, 7, 10, 13, and 15. (Instrument recordings attached.)

Personal Observations: DW-19 is a small world. According to the calculations of One Alone (which agree with those of former expeditions) she is just large enough to be able to hold her atmosphere. I have decided to concentrate on DW-19 because she is, without doubt, the most enigmatic of all of the Dead Worlds. Her star is the focal point of the sac. She is central to the other nineteen worlds and it has been theorized that she is the home planet of the sac worlds.

Why is she the most enigmatic? Because I can look out the viewport and see cloud formations on the day side. There is a large cyclonic storm in the southern portion of a great ocean, and I can see the gleam of an ice cap at the north pole. If I didn't know exactly where I am, I would think that I was in orbit around a home system world, and that upon landing I would encounter civilization. DW-19 is a beauty, and there's no scientific or logical reason for her to have an oxygen atmosphere without having vegetation or life in her seas. Just as it is difficult to explain why DW-I is cold to the core, it's tough to guess how DW-19 developed an oxygen-nitrogen-water vapor atmosphere.

If the United Planets Department of Exploration and Alien Search had not zoned the sac for scientific study only, DW-19 could be colonized, if you could find someone willing to live on a ghost world. The construction machines just might turn up something that we wouldn't want to see—the skeleton of one of the former residents, perhaps. I, for one, would love to see that happen. I'd like to know what sort of being it was who left behind only a threat against all comers.

There is an eerie feeling on DW-19, more than on any other Dead World. I don't think any rational human being would want to live anywhere in this sac system. There are too damned many stars too close. The nights are too bright. Multiple suns confuse man's biological clock. After a while, I think you'd begin to feel like a bug living under a battery of floodlights.

DW-19 has a complex orbit influenced by her primary sun, DW-H, by her secondary sun, DW-J, and in minor but fascinating ways—at least they are interesting to One Alone—by all of the other suns in the sac. She has no winter except in the polar regions of the north, where the energy of the sun DW-J does not reach. She should have life. Every water world yet discovered has some form of life, mainly vegetation and microscopic organisms.

We are taking the usual precautions before landing on DW-19. The whole ship is undergoing sterilization. The landing site we have chosen is on the western massif of the equatorial land mass. The maps made by the Sparks expedition show accumulations of eroded rubble in the mountain valleys. A sizable city is sited a few miles away on the plain. We feel that our best chances of making any new discovery will be in the mountains. They're quite rugged in places. We're guessing that the very inaccessibility of some of the mountain areas might be a plus, that some sites may have been overlooked by previous expeditions.

Our first serious dig will be made at Map Site W-2, P-45.55, Sparks Expedition Map 22. The first military expedition, some fourteen thousand years ago, reported traces of heavy metals at that site. Their data has been disputed by later expeditions. We've got the latest heavy metal detecting equipment aboard *Paulus,* so our first goal will be to try to confirm the early expedition's findings.

NOTE: Restrictions on these personal observations are the same as previously stated.

This is a funny world, this DW-19. The land mass girds the equator as if the centrifugal force of the planet's rotation collected great masses of molten rock into an equatorial band. It would be possible to walk on land around this world. If given the chance, Clear Thought might try it since Healers are big on walking.

Aside from the fact that we can work without space armor on DW-19, I chose her for another reason. Pure hunch. She's been examined more thoroughly than some of the less hospitable worlds in the sac, but she's still my choice. The Old Earthers have been checking her out from orbit. One Alone's senses can tell me more about a planet in an hour than all of our electronic instruments can in a week.

Stella has programmed a complete diagram of the planet's magnetic and gravitational fields into the computer. There are some peculiarities since the planet is influenced strongly by two suns plus the other sac stars. There are some interesting displays of magnetic interference at the poles.

One Alone says that he has not observed anything of note not recorded by previous expeditions. Clear Thought is eager to be traveling under his own power on the surface. He stalks the lounge, eager to feel the ground under his armored feet.

Cecile, the sunny one, seems to be apprehensive, but aren't we all? I am not afraid of that world down there. What I fear most is failure. I do not want to eke out a degree from Xanthos University merely by confirming past observations. It would be easy enough to fake a lengthy thesis simply by cross-referencing old data with new, but I do not want to settle for that. I am determined to add new knowledge about this odd and eerie place. I refuse to believe that there are not clues to be found. Clues to something—to the physical shape of the inhabitants, to the degree of technological advancement, clues to something.

What I would like to do is piece together threads of evidence that would give us a portrait of the planet killers, or, at worst, of the people of these worlds if the killers and the inhabitants were not the same. I will not accept mere confirmation of recorded data. I will not contemplate failure. If I have to dig down to the core of this world, turn over every rock, sift every ounce of rubble, I will do so. We have the most sophisticated equipment and machines. We have manpower. We will not fail. We will take something of value back to Xanthos, something that will set the scientific community on its ear. I promise all this to myself, for no lesser result would be acceptable to a Tigian.

CHAPTER SEVEN

It was not possible to determine exactly how much of the rugged rocks that made up the mountains had been denuded of vegetation and topsoil at the time of the destruction. There was evidence of thousands of years of erosion. Sterile rain had sculpted vast canyons and had piled detritus at the bottom of slopes and hills.

Temperatures were cool on the seven-thousand-foot slopes, steamy on the plain. The air was sweet, fouled only by the dust created by the *Paulus* expedition. It seemed odd to be working in a rich, heady oxygen atmosphere where the only natural sound was that of the wind. No insect hummed or chirped. There was no flap of wing, no territorial bird calls, no scurry of tiny feet. There were no trees, no grass, no weeds. The only life on the planet had come down to the surface in the scouts from *Paulus*.

It took several trips to put all of the heavy equipment on the ground. Two portable huts were set up, complete with life-support systems which were not needed in the sweet, pure air of DW-19. A high speed surface crawler made the trip down from orbit lashed into place piggyback on one of the scouts. Each of the small vessels was equipped with an external grappler for handling heavy equipment either in space or at the bottom of a planet's gravity well. Back on Xanthos they had practiced with all of the equipment so that there were no delays in setting it up before an evening shower moved up from the southwest. Inside the huts weather control turned on heaters to counteract the damp chill of rain at a seven-thousand-foot elevation.

A bald, eroded peak rose a thousand feet into the sky behind the camp. The huts had been set up on a wide, rock ledge at the top of an eroded slope. Below was a v-shaped valley filled by centuries of erosion product. LaConius believed that the rubble under the overburden of rocks and soil would be virgin.

To the east, past the foothills and the narrow plain, was the ocean. It reflected the blue of the sky. As evening fell, blue turned to slate and then blackness as the dense star fields of the core emerged.

Clear Thought stayed outside when the others went in to escape the evening chill. He stood with his head back, his eyes widened to maximum, his ears attuned to the silence. Long confinement aboard *Paulus* had made him restless. He left the camp, taking long, ground-covering strides, climbed obliquely upward toward the peak that towered over the camp. Loose rocks skittered and rolled under his feet and clattered down the slope.

A Healer's eyes had been evolved to be effective in the murky atmosphere of Old Earth. In pristine air, Clear Thought's vision was superhuman.

He stood alone on the peak, felt a pleasant tiredness in his neglected leg muscles, breathed in great gulps of pure air so rich in oxygen that it made him heady. There was a beauty in the night with the stars so close that the nearest of them were visible as disks against the solid pearl glow of the core. He turned, letting his eyes search the sky and the dark, rugged mountains below his perch atop the peak. Something teased his senses, something indefinable. There was a quality to the movement of air past his scales that eluded him.

He sent his thoughts winging upward toward the orbiting *Paulus.* "One Alone, share with me."

He felt the brush of the Far Seer's mind. He stood motionless. His massive lungs were filled with air. His blood was so saturated with oxygen that he had no need to breathe. His gills were closed. He blanked his mind and let his senses take over, searching for that elusive something that was just beyond reach. A small moon rose in the east, reflected the overall luminosity of the sky. The satellite moved five, ten degrees and still the Healer was motionless.

"There is nothing that can be isolated," One Alone said finally. "The others will wonder where you are."

As if on cue, Stella called. He gave her a view from the peak as he ran down the slope in long bounds, reveling in the stretch and pull of his muscles.

CHAPTER EIGHT

Shapeless bits of stone, metal, and glass had been collected by every expedition that had visited the Dead Worlds. Under the accumulation of detritus in the valley was a layer of rubble which offered the *Paulus* expedition the same old challenge, to find a fragment of material large enough or distinct enough to give information about those who had made it. Metals had been melted into shapeless, tiny blobs. Glass, most often, was fused with sand or rock.

Highly trained archaeologists and scientists of all disciplines had studied the evidence long before any of the members of the *Paulus* expedition were born. The rubble fields of DW-19 were carefully cataloged. The Sparks Expedition had left permanent plaques at all of the major sites. The plaques listed the names of the members of the expedition and gave a brief summary of the results of the digs.

On the lower slope below the campsite Sparks had cleared rubble from a mine. To check the efficiency and thoroughness of those who had cleared the shaft, LaConius used a mine bore to clear away massive rockfalls. There was still some debris in the mine, but nothing else. Not to be outdone by Sparks, he left a plaque on the wall of the shaft at its deepest point telling of *his* work.

In the foothills were streams of pure water which, in the past, had attracted habitation. The banks of the streams had many small rubble fields to indicate past occupation. The planet had been thickly populated.

To a dedicated archaeologist the expedition's use of modern tools would have been labeled heresy. LaConius was especially pleased with the results of using a tool that had been developed as a weapon of war, the disassembler. The small, compact machine destroyed everything touched by its adjustable beam, reducing the material to its individual atoms to be swept away invisibly. With the disassembler it was possible to remove megatons of silt and detritus and expose the ancient rubble.

"We have to be damned careful with this thing," LaConius warned.

"Rank has its privileges," Cecile said. "If old Cone weren't the son of the president of a rich and powerful planetary grouping, we'd be removing this stuff by hand, or, at best, with the automated diggers."

The disassembler was mounted on the prow of the land crawler. It allowed examination of representative areas in the valley. When those excavations revealed only the usual unidentifiable rubble, John drove the crawler toward the city on the plain while the others hopped over in the scouts. The camp was left in place, for it was cool on the slope and it was only minutes to the selected city site.

The location of the city indicated that those who had built it were oriented toward the sea. Arms of land enclosed a sheltered harbor. Clear Thought, whose armor and lung capacity made him a very effective underwater explorer, tested the harbor bottom and found traces of rubble in the mud.

Dust and silt had reclaimed the excavations of the past. This shallow surface overlay was swept aside by the disassembler set on wide beam for low penetration. Some of the old digs had been made very neatly. Others were hasty and sloppy, as if the diggers had become impatient or disillusioned.

The city site exposed the only evidence of building technique known on the twenty worlds. The Sparks expedition had discovered foundation members sunk into bedrock. The pilings were square, and their composition was similar to ordinary cement. A ferrous metal reinforcement had long since oxidized into a fine, rusty powder. The cementlike pilings had generated much speculation, with Sparks going so far as to attribute humanoid shapes to those who had built them.

It was the consensus of the group to go deeper than any previous expedition. This decision was inspired by digs on Old Earth that were uncovering an astounding variety of artifacts ranging from stone tools in the lower levels to sophisticated metal alloys nearer the surface. On DW-19 it was hoped that deep excavations would reach back into the planet's prehistory. One stone arrowhead would tell more about the people of the planet than was currently known.

Several clean cuts were made by the disassembler to a depth of ninety feet. The results were disappointing. In places the overlay of rubble was ten feet thick. Under the rubble was a shallow layer of soil. From depths of ten to fifteen feet on down, there was only bedrock.

"If we accept this," LaConius said, as he guided the disassembler through the overburden of rubble, "we'll have to say that all the archaeological evidence indicates that intelligent life existed for only a brief period of time."

"Perhaps the city was built on a virgin site," John suggested.

"Sure," LaConius said. "And so were all the other sites on all twenty worlds."

"It is puzzling," Clear Thought said. "But all of the previous expeditions reported the same enigma."

On all of the worlds where the evidence had not been completely erased, as it had been on DW-I, the areas of habitation had been constructed on sites that showed no hints of previous use. The only conclusion to be drawn was that civilization and technology had developed in what was, in archaeological time, one swift, magical moment.

In spite of the most modern machines, there was still tedious hand work to be done. Day after day sifted materials from the rubble layer were examined minutely, with uniformly disappointing results. Metals, including gold, silver, and platinum, were found, but in melted bits of slag that gave no clue as to their former shapes.

The group had been divided into two teams. One team consisted of LaConius, John, and Cecile. The other was composed of Clear Thought, Stella, and Martha. Clear Thought turned his attention back to the bottom of the harbor after several days of tedious digging, sifting, testing, and sorting. He could seal off his lungs and withstand pressures that would have required an Old One to wear protective gear. His eyes were double-lidded so that he could close his inner lids and protect his eyes. He worked diligently, but the silt-covered rubble of the harbor bottom was as thoroughly pulverized as that on land.

After a long, hot day's work it was pleasant to return to the mountain camp. There the weather was like spring on a sensible planet and the showers worked well. The huts were cozy, the conversation was usually lively, but the moment of greatest excitement came when Martha developed the sniffles, indicating that somehow a cold virus had managed to evade the sterilization of the *Paulus*. Equipment was rushed down from the orbiting ship and after Martha was cured, a thorough scan of the huts failed to turn up any free virus.

During the long evenings, those who were not too tired played an antique gambling game that had been brought out from Old Earth by the original space trekkers. They played with varying skills. Clear Thought and Stella, who could easily have cheated by reading the thoughts of their friends, played on their honor. Clear Thought was almost always a winner, and taking his winnings made him feel guilty. Cecile was a chump for the most obvious of bluffs. Bits of precious metals recovered from the sifters were used as money, with the understanding that all artifacts, however insignificant, would be returned to the ship's collection in the end.

On a night of seasonal change brought on by the tilt of the planet to the nearest of its two suns, Clear Thought ran what was, to all but Cecile, an obvious bluff. She threw in what would have been the winning hand and lost the last of her stake.

"That's it," she said. "I'm leaving you professional gamblers."

"If you're going outside," Martha said, "you'd better take a wrap. It's cold."

"Would you mind company?" Clear Thought asked.

"Not at all," Cecile said. "Come along."

Clear Thought spent a lot of time out of doors at night. As a child he had lived underneath a sky so murky that only the special senses of a Far Seer could detect the stars. He still remembered his first un-clouded look at space and the stars, as a U.P. troopship lifted him and hundreds of others off the dying Earth. He was in constant awe of the massed millions of stars that made up the core of the galaxy. He would spend hours on the peak, lying flat on his back to watch the wheeling of the glowing masses in the heavens of DW-19. He also liked watching the planet's small moon. It was low on the horizon, made dim by the glow of the stars, when he and Cecile came out of the hut.

One Alone was analyzing the change of seasons, sharing his thoughts with both Clear Thought and Stella. "The net effect will be," he said, "a slight de-crease of temperatures in the lowlands and a lessening of the showers, accompanied by freezing temperatures in the mountains. The ocean tides will be higher for a few weeks as the primary and its close neighbor come into conjunction with the moon."

"That will be interesting," Clear Thought sent back.

Cecile walked at his side until the music and the voices from the hut became faint. There was no wind.

"It's an unnatural silence," Cecile said. She shivered.

"Cold?" Clear Thought asked.

"Not really. Total silence is so damned lonely." She

touched Clear Thought's arm as if for comfort. He patted her hand.

"Wouldn't it be great to be able to soar like Stella?" Cecile asked. "I'd like to be able to look down on the ocean and see the starlight reflected."

"That would be beautiful," Clear Thought agreed.

"If only there were just a few sounds," she said. "A bird. A small animal hunting in the night." She laughed. "I'll probably stay awake the first night I'm back in Xanthos City just to listen to the ground traffic sounds."

"Homesick?" Clear Thought asked.

"Only at night. I'm fine during the day when we're working. I think we're doing something worthwhile, even if we haven't produced spectacular results yet. I'm naturally an optimist in the sunlight. During the day I firmly believe we're going to pull a secret or two out of this world and then when night comes I feel myself falling into the negative. I catalog little blobs of metal and ask the same questions over and over. What power did they use to do such a total job of destruction? Why is there gold, silver, and platinum, but no copper? They drove pilings into bedrock, indicating that they built a pretty impressive city, that they had at least early industrial development. But there's no sign that they had electricity. No copper for wiring—"

"Maybe gold and silver were so plentiful that they used them," Clear Thought said.

"That's a thought, but if so I'd think we'd find more of each."

"Sparks theorized that they used solar power."

"We may be underestimating them," Cecile said. "Maybe they had broadcast power."

"But no atomics," Clear Thought said. "It was every-one's first guess that nuclear weapons reduced the planets, but there's no evidence of that. I was reading the old records just last night to see if there was any in-dication that they had ever mined uranium. The ship's probes show pretty sizable deposits of it, but there's no sign of a nuclear culture. If they had developed newks and used them, these worlds would still glow in the dark. When it comes to some of the meaner man-generated radioactive particles, 75,000 years isn't even half-life."

"Are you going to put a study of radioactivity into your thesis?" Cecile asked.

"Perhaps," he said. "Right now it's shaping up to be an addendum to the thousands and thousands of pages of speculation already written."

They stood on the edge of a steep drop and looked toward the sea. When Cecile spoke, it was with convic-tion. "Something had to survive. A button. A needle. A coin. On one of our older worlds you can dig down through the past and read it like a book. You can date each level. The deeper you dig, the farther back in time you go. The things that people leave behind them to be covered by earth tell us about them. Here you dig down ninety feet and there are only two levels, three, at the most. Rubble. Soil. Bedrock. They sprang into be-ing and disappeared in one incredibly brief burst of ac-tivity. There are no primitive artifacts, no evidence of a pre-stone age or a stone age or an iron age. There's just nothing, and then there is devastation."

"I visited John's planet on a summer vacation once," Clear Thought said. "There and on other worlds artists have carved mountains into works of beauty or of commemoration of some hero. I've wondered why there's no evidence of monumental works here."

"Either they had no heroes or the destruction erased the evidence."

"But how would you destroy a mountain sculpted into the bust of a hero?"

"How did the destruction extend to the mud of the bottom of the sea?" she countered. "What force would be required to pulverize an artifact lying in two hundred feet of water?"

"It would have to be a form of energy unknown to us."

"When Earth was first rediscovered," Cecile said, "and the media began to tell the U.P. worlds about your people, about the powers of the Far Seers and how you all could read minds, there was some fear that you were superhuman and that you would conquer all. There was some hysteria about the powers of the mind, and the dangers thereof."

"We can send thoughts," Clear Thought said. "Far Seers can affect a biological system, even at great distance."

"Could One Alone kill if he so desired?"

"You know the answer to that," Clear Thought said.

"I know what I've heard, and what I've read. I've never asked an Old Earther straight out if a Far Seer can kill with his mind."

"Yes," Clear Thought said, "but a Far Seer is born with such a concentrated reverence for life that no Seer has ever used his power of life and death."

"A new form of energy?" Cecile asked.

"Not powerful enough to shatter metal objects into fragments and melt the fragments into slag. Not powerful enough to crumble stone. Not enough to cool the core of a world and kill billions of living beings."

Cecile seemed to accept the disclaimer. "Will we find anything?" she asked. "Or will we have to be content with writing papers that present nothing new and accept our degrees like a child being patted on the head." She lisped sweetly. "Very good, kiddies. You've done well. Now go forth into society and do something useful."

Clear Thought laughed. "What useful activity do you plan when you go out into society?"

"I have pictured myself as Dr. Cecile of Xanthos University, explorer, one of those who deciphered the mystery of the Dead Worlds."

"Sounds good," Clear Thought said.

The moon had climbed thirty degrees above the horizon and was a dim globe against the glory of the vast fields of core stars.

"Beautiful," Cecile said. "But terrible, too. It makes me want to hold an umbrella over my head. I know it's silly, but I feel unprotected."

"Perhaps your sixth sense is warning you," Clear Thought said.

"Warning me? Of what?"

"It's nothing to worry about on a short-term basis," he said, "but cosmic ray activity is much heavier here."

"Ugh," she said, imagining cosmic bullets piercing her soft flesh. "You can feel them, can't you?"

"Yes," he said. The rays made little pinging sounds on his scales. He examined his body, sweeping countless billions of cells quickly. Cecile turned and started walking back toward the huts. She was about fifty paces away when the northern sky blossomed with cold fire.

A glow grew from below the horizon and erupted upward to encompass a quarter of the sky. Clear Thought saw Cecile halt and lift her head to the multihued glory of the display. Streamers of flame flickered toward the zenith. The planet was crowned by a mantle of color and as Clear Thought projected mind pictures to One Alone, wisps of color reached outward toward the dim moon.

"Stella, quickly," Clear Thought sent. The rainbow of color in the northern half of the sky exploded and shattered and re-formed, dimming the pearl glow of the stars.

"I observe," One Alone sent from his stateroom aboard *Paulus*.

Stella was moving quickly toward the door of the hut. She joined her mind to Clear Thought's, seeing with his eyes.

"It seems to be electromagnetic," Stella said. "A function of the magnetic field. Do you agree, One Alone?"

"Similar displays have been observed on other planets," One Alone said, "but not, to my knowledge, of this intensity."

"Is there danger of damage to the Old Ones?" Clear Thought asked, for Cecile was still standing with her face toward the sky, watching in awe. "I sense no damaging radiation."

"There is no immediate danger," One Alone said. "I will report further as *Paulus* orbits through the aurora."

The hut door burst open just as the light in the sky faded and disappeared even more rapidly than it had appeared. The flare of color had lasted less than a minute. *Paulus* had been approaching the upper streamers of the display when they ceased to exist.

Clear Thought used mind pictures to show John, Martha, and LaConius what they had missed. One Alone reported that there was still measurable agitation in the planet's magnetic field. The recorders aboard *Paulus* had operated automatically to capture the display. The group gathered in one hut to watch a replay on a viewer.

"Pretty," LaConius said.

"It's something new, Cone," Cecile said. "I just ran a cross-reference search through the computer. No other expedition saw such a display."

"Well, it's something," LaConius said, "even if there are hundreds of planets that have polar auroras."

The following day was devoted to routine work. In the evening the nightly poker game got under way and immediately Cecile had an incredible run of luck. She played her hands to the best possible advantage. She refused to fall for a bluff from Clear Thought and raked in the pot. Not once but several times she folded rather strong hands in the face of hands that were even stronger. She ran unpredictable bluffs that convinced everyone. On the last hand of the night, the one with which she cleaned out the remaining players, she raised holding nothing but a pair of tens against four hearts showing toward a flush.

"How in the world did you have the guts to stay with a single pair against an obvious flush?" John demanded.

"It wasn't obvious," she said, with a little shrug. "What was obvious was that the down card was black."

To prove that it wasn't a fluke, she was the big winner on the following night. Martha was the last to go.

She threw in a losing hand in disgust and said, "She's a card sharp. All this time she's been setting us up, pretending to be a terrible player."

Cecile looked thoughtful. "I was a pretty lousy player, wasn't I?"

"Who always was the first to lose it all?" Martha asked.

"Me," Cecile said.

"So what has changed?" John asked.

"I don't know," Cecile said. "All of a sudden I just *know*. I know that when you raise you're just trying to run me out so that I won't have a chance to draw the third card for three of a kind. I know when someone is hoping to fill out two pairs."

"You know what we've got in our hands?" LaConius asked. "Is One Alone helping you?"

"That is negative," One Alone sent.

"It's just a run of luck, I guess," Cecile said. "I'll probably lose next time."

"What next time, card sharp?" LaConius said teasingly.

"Well, I'll give it back," Cecile said, pushing her pile of metal bits toward the center of the table.

LaConius gathered the pile between his hands, smirked, and said, "Mine, all mine."

Cecile laughed. "Stick with me, pal, and I'll make you rich."

Clear Thought's face could not show amusement, nor did he feel like saying, "Smile." He was studying Cecile's face, feeling the force of her thoughts.

"Yes," One Alone said to Clear Thought, "there is a difference."

CHAPTER NINE

I, One Alone, store these thoughts with my Keeper. Idle digressions are restricted to personal retrieval pending future deletion.

You sleep so sweetly, my Dear Companion. You are serenely untroubled by recent events. You lie supine before me with your long, slim legs twitching occasionally with the dream that flickers dimly in that tiny, private segment of your brain. I use the words of the Old Ones. I look at you. I see you. I speak as if I had those organs called eyes, but I look with my heart—to use an abstraction of the Old Ones—with my senses to know your softness and your sweetness.

Few who have eyes have looked upon you, for they would see only your imperfections. They would see the slackness of muscle, the fleshly formlessness of a creature who is nominally female. They would see a distorted imitation of the women of the Old Ones and wonder how those of your kind, soft and unprotected, survived to live and become an integral part of our society. They would feel only pity for your paucity of fine motor control, for the eternal infancy of your mind and your personality. Only a Far Seer can know the hidden beauty and the innate and infinite sensuality of a Keeper.

While it is true that other Old Earthers have access to your storehouse of data with my permission, the New Ones, with the honorable but intrusive motives of the do-gooder, would say, perhaps, that you are used unfairly, that you could and should be replaced by one of their computers, but how little they know. You and your kind are the greatest treasure of our race, for stored away in the areas of your large brain that are inaccessible to you are tradition, history, the moral code by which we live, and all things recorded since the time following the Destruction.

I am content to listen to your sleep sounds while my mind idles. I touch you and there is a smile on your face and in your hips a hint of those movements to which my body is so well attuned. In contrast to the life span of a Far Seer, my Dear Companion, we have been together only briefly, you and I. I mature, but your smooth face is untouched. You retain your youthful softness. I know, and the knowledge is sweet, how you reach for me in your un-coordinated way when I awaken you, for Nature created you for me and made me for you. In Her wisdom she made Keepers and Far Seers one, indivisible, mutually de-pendent. She took my eyes and gave me mental expan-sion. She deprived you of mental growth and gave you your heady appreciation of pleasure. Perhaps, poor Na-ture, she had few gifts remaining after creating Healers and Power Givers, but there is no envy in me. I would be nothing but what I am with you beside me.

We are alone, you and I, encased in a construction of metals, suspended on high where with a sweep of senses I can study more stars, more worlds than were dreamed of by our Seers before the Reunification. You and I are one with Nature, with the universe.

All is quiet below. The games are over for the night. Voices are silent as the moon sinks and the planet spins on its axis and the stars swing so slowly, slowly, in their appointed arcs. The winds of their burning are confused, difficult to distinguish individually.

Well, to work. I search. I send my mind outward to measure and I insert into your brain the findings to become a part of my permanent record. At least as permanent as you and I are.

I sense that something has changed. It is an undefined and very subtle difference in the feel of the closely crowded vastness of the fields of core area stars. Am I sensing the power of the blackness at the center of the galaxy? If so, I cannot separate it from the interlaced, overlapping, and muddled streams of the solar winds.

Stella feels the change. Clear Thought has not yet detected it, although he was outside when the aurora filled the northern sky. Of the Old Ones, only Cecile was directly exposed. The others were protected by the radiation shields of the huts.

So it is Cecile who is to be studied. I insert the encephalic waves of Cecile of Xanthos and compare them with previously recorded readings. The comparison shows a slight bending of pre-thought impulses in the cerebral cortex adjacent to the occipital regions. The altered impulses bear a superficial resemblance to those present in the brain of a soaring Power Giver.

Although we will not speak of this as yet, lest we cause needless concern, we will monitor continuously to determine whether the altered brain waves are the symptom of a temporary condition engendered, perhaps, by the stimulation of the aurora.

Had it not been for Cecile's sudden mastery of the Old

Ones' card game I would have been less interested in the minor variations of her brain waves. If she had developed game skills slowly, I would have attributed it to a learning process. It is the sudden change that fascinates me.

It is good that the rules of privacy were suspended for the duration of this expedition. I am able to read Cecile as she sleeps. I see no reason for concern.

Tomorrow I will conduct waking examinations of all members of the expedition. I will ask LaConius to prohibit exposure to any unusual fields, such as the aurora, until we know more.

Now I sort information, repeating previous examinations of data. Sleep is near as I, linked mentally with my Dear Companion, give myself ease and share the knowledge of the past with all those who have gone before me. Ah, the thoughts of the great ones, of Rack the Healer, and ancient Rose. Good. Good. But I sense a restlessness in my Dear Companion.

She wakes. I tend her, and, having restored her comfort, my blood heats and drives from my mind my resolve not to disturb her sleep.

Ah, you awaken, my Dear Companion.

CHAPTER TEN

"There has to be more to life than this," John said. He mopped his face with a large handkerchief already stained by the dark earth of the dig. He sat down on a pile of rubble.

"Less talk, more work," LaConius said.

"I'm tired of looking down," John said. "Think about it. Our primitive ancestor on Old Earth learns to walk on his hind legs. In standing erect, he's nearer the sky, closer to the sun and the stars and the moon. So what does he do? He looks down to find something on the ground—the spoor of game, berries on low growing vines, flint for his weapons. He looks down because he's always trying to get something for nothing. He's shiftless. From the very beginning he's nothing more than a treasure hunter."

"He looked up at times," LaConius said.

"Not much," John said. "It takes less energy to look down. It works more muscles to hold your head erect when you're walking."

"Maybe he was just used to looking at the ground," LaConius said. "After all, he'd been going around on all fours for a long time. He learned to look up because a lot of his food grew on trees."

"Maybe, but as soon as he had eaten he looked back down to the ground."

"Oh, hell," LaConius said.

"He was looking for diamonds."

"He had no use for diamonds then," LaConius said in exasperation.

"Sure he did. Evolution gave him a hand with an opposing thumb and such a biological construction demands something to hold, something that pleases the eye, something shining and pretty. A diamond."

"You're full of it, John," LaConius said. "A diamond in the rough isn't pretty at all."

"Maybe at first it was just a colorful pebble," John said. "It was, of course, something natural, something fashioned by nature. It was only later that the hand began to work in conjunction with the brain to fashion artifacts. Then hand got lazy and grew tired of the tedious work of chipping flint. Brain told hand, 'Hey, look for something that some other hand has made.' Thus archaeology was born."

"The lad's a genius," Martha said.

"Here we are," John went on, "with the whole galaxy out there just begging to be explored. We have supplies and food for years. We have an unlimited source of power. So what do we do? We dig in the dirt hoping to find some object made by someone else's hand."

"That's an oversimplification, of course," LaConius said.

"We are not treasure hunting," Martha said. "Because we're not looking for something which can be sold for money."

"Money is only a form of exchange," John said, "and, as old Cone has pointed out, it takes on an entirely different character when there's enough of it. It becomes a symbol of power, a way of keeping score. We're not here trying to turn something into money? Ha. What will a terminal degree do for each of us? It will increase our earning power, and we all need that except old Cone, here. When we find something new, something made by the hands of the dead who once lived here, we'll put it on display in the Alien Exhibits Room at the university museum with a plaque on which is engraved our names. In effect, we will be exchanging the artifact for recognition, which translates into money in the marketplace."

"With a stroke of his deadly tongue the poet discredits the science of archaeology," LaConius said.

"And other ologies as well," Martha said.

"So you agree?" John asked.

"To a point," Martha said.

"Our first goal is to invent a reason for being here where so much work has already been done. We have this opportunity because of Cone's money. It isn't just any student who can mount a space expedition. We search in the dirt for justification for the expenditure of Tigian money. Primarily, we're digging for a piece of paper, a paper that says John of Selbelle III has completed the work necessary to earn a terminal degree in the science of—what? That paper will be a personal treasure because it will bring me money. What we're doing bears direct correlation to the prospector who rambles off into space in a patched up old space tug in search of gold or diamonds."

"John," Laconius said, "work drives idle thoughts from the mind. Try it."

John sighed, picked up his shovel. "Actually, I've had it with this particular spot."

"I hear you," LaConius said. "I guess it's time to move on."

"Where?" Martha asked. "Every known site on the twenty planets has been explored a dozen times or more."

"Any suggestions?" LaConius asked.

"Somewhere where something will happen," John said. "Somewhere where we will find something to give us a clue to these people."

"Where?" LaConius asked, spreading his hands helplessly.

"I don't know," John said.

The virus of discontent was contagious. LaConius had difficulty organizing the nightly poker game. Cecile, Stella, and John were poring over maps of digs by former expeditions. Martha was uncharacteristically restless to the point of being somewhat irritable. She set up a holo-projector and began to study slides at random. Views of the sac system were projected in the air.

The stars of the Dead Worlds system formed a complicated pattern. The sac was a lopsided square, with one star offset toward the core of the galaxy. Around the stars orbited thirty-one planets, a concentration unique in the explored areas of the galaxy. Not only were there an unprecedented number of planets—ice worlds, gas giants, sun-scorched orbs of rock—but a surprisingly high percentage of them were in the life zone.

Each star in the sac was influenced by all others. There was an intricate interlacing of orbits as star circled star. The planets swam paths controlled by a primary and, most often, at least one secondary sun. Some planets had multiple seasons. When Martha increased the speed of the projection, the planets raced through odd ellipses, bobbing and weaving in a frantic dance as they came under the gravitational influences of neighboring stars.

The central mass of the galaxy, concentrated so closely by cosmic standards, affected the entire system, acted on each individual star, each single world, making it more difficult to chart and predict the orbital and spatial movements of the units within the sac. To make it even more complicated, the gravitational unit that was the sac system had satellites in the form of stars and star groups.

"An astrologer would go nuts here," Cecile said. "How would you like to try to draw a chart taking into account the influence of over fifty astrological bodies, not counting the moons?"

"I want to see the dean's face when you turn in a thesis on the astrological complications in the Dead World Sac," LaConius said.

"On Selbelle III that would be considered a serious subject worthy of study," John said.

"You're kidding me," LaConius said.

"Not at all," John said. "There is an active cult. All of the old myths have been collected. The media run daily horoscopes. Not everyone is a believer, but a lot of people think it's sort of fun to read what the stars predict for them each morning."

"I sometimes wonder about our ancestors," Martha said. "They forgot the location of their world of origin but they preserved complex bodies of folklore, such as the astrological signs. When Bradley Gore rediscovered

Old Earth one of the proofs cited that it was, indeed, the planet of origin was that the planet's heavens matched the Zodiacal Belt."

"Consider this," John said. "Selbelle VI doesn't have a moon, but the astrologers speak of the moon's influence on daily activities."

"It is not all superstition." One Alone's words came to all of them simultaneously. "Man is influenced by the movement of heavenly bodies."

Cecile could not resist the impulse to look up toward the point where *Paulus* rode in a stationary orbit above them.

"Senses that are developed only in a Far Seer register the most minute gravitational changes," One Alone said. "Stella is sensitive to the magnetic field of a world. She can tell you the position of this planet's moon at any given moment."

"Maybe we should ask you to draw up an astrological chart for DW-19," LaConius said.

"Not specifically a zodiac," One Alone said, "but I do, of course, chart and measure the fluctuations of the various gravitational fields as the system performs its various movements through space. It is a complicated and interesting study."

LaConius winked at John. "Well, keep up the good work, One Alone," he said.

Far Seers were not noted for a sense of humor. "I don't consider it to be work," One Alone said, "but I will, of course, continue."

Cecile made a face at LaConius and giggled.

LaConius came to his feet. "Let's get out of this damned hut," he said. "Let's do a flyover of this whole bedamned planet."

"Can't that wait until morning?" Stella asked.

"I suppose so," LaConius said. "Any volunteers?"

There were. It was unanimous. The flyover project took up four days. The scouts flashed around the world, flying low with all sensors working. When the job was finished, another day was spent in checking the readings.

Clear Thought concentrated on studying the planet's ore concentrations. He concluded that the metallic resources had hardly been touched. Iron ore seemed to have been the most heavily mined. Rich deposits of uranium had not been touched. There were, however, interesting depletions of fossil fuel deposits near the surface. Coal had been dug. Oil had been pumped from salt domes.

LaConius was glum. "All that is in the account left by Sparks. He concluded that the fossil fuel stage of development was limited to a brief period, that the society turned quickly to another source of power."

"Which he didn't identify," Clear Thought said.

"It's interesting that there are no traces of a transportation system," Martha said.

"Sparks commented on that, too," LaConius said. "He speculated that there was no permanent construction, such as massive metal bridges, railroads, or paved roads during the fossil fuel stage of development. After that he had no guesses."

"No roads, or there'd be lines of rubble," Cecile said. "No rails. No airports. No launch pads."

"They were in space," Clear Thought said. "To ask that we accept that civilization evolved simultaneously on twenty worlds is absurd."

"What if the Dead Worlds were not the original

home of the people who inhabited them?" Cecile asked. "There are no primitive artifacts, remember? We have only two worlds to use as standards, Old Earth and the Artounee planet. On each of them intelligence developed slowly, beginning with the evidence of stone tools. Here, there is no transition from the primitive to what was, at least, an early industrial society. Both the Artounee and the people of Old Earth had stone weapons and tools and then learned to work metals."

"You've got a point," LaConius said. "A race just doesn't suddenly evolve into mining the earth, refining metals—"

"And traveling in space," Clear Thought added.

"The same questions have been posed before," John said.

"I don't want to hear that," Cecile said with a smile.

"Sorry," John said, "read the Borden papers, lady."

"A pox on Borden and all the others," Cecile said.

"If they didn't originate here," Martha asked, "where?"

"In there," John said, indicating the core light that glowed in through an open window.

"Or out there," LaConius said, pointing outward toward the distant periphery.

Martha shivered as she envisioned intergalactic emptiness and the distant galaxies.

"Build not," LaConius said. "For we shall return." He spread his hands. "If they were nearby, somewhere in this galaxy, wouldn't they have already noted that for fifteen thousand years people have been messing around in the sac?"

"No one has built," Cecile said.

"When they said 'we shall return' did that mean that

they had come once before or that they were just leaving?" Martha asked.

"You tell me," John said.

"No life-form could exist much closer to the core than this," Clear Thought said.

"No life-form we know," Cecile said.

"An energy form," Stella said. "Pure energy. Magnificently powerful. Unaffected by the radiation storms."

"Able to zap in and out of a black hole," John said.

"Ellington postulated a life-form based on quartzlike crystals," Martha said. "Such a life-form could withstand heat and radiation that would turn rock molten."

"Are the blobs of melted glass in the rubble the bones of the natives?" Cecile asked.

John laughed. "They came in different colors."

"I think the conversation is disintegrating," LaConius said. "We have to decide what we're going to do next."

With a suddenness that was always disturbing One Alone was in their minds. "Stella and Clear Thought only," he said. "Outside."

Stella and Clear Thought obeyed instantly.

"What's happening?" LaConius asked, leaping to his feet.

"All others don protective armor," One Alone ordered.

"The aurora," Cecile said, running toward the door.

"One Alone said put on gear," LaConius yelled.

Cecile ignored him. She followed the Old Earthers out. The door slammed behind her. The others struggled into space armor.

The sky was alive. Color in thrilling, vibrant intensity writhed upward, exploding into showers of brightness. It was a splendor that hurt the eyes. Cecile stood with her head back, her hair blowing in the wind, her mouth open. The colors in the sky were reflected in her green eyes.

Stella was measuring the disturbance in the magnetic field of the planet. John turned on a light recorder.

"From the air, Stella," One Alone said.

Stella soared, glanced down from a height of a thousand feet, then turned her eyes back to the aurora as she accelerated into cooling, thinning air. She felt the shifting distortions in the magnetic field. She sent her observations directly into the brain of Dear Companion even as she angled northward, climbing until her lungs strained to sift out stray atoms of oxygen. In her eagerness she was using the substance of her body as fuel.

The colors intensified to lush richness and streamers lashed outward into near space. They seemed to form a semiliquid mass near the surface to the north. A rainbow oozed southward toward the equator, burst, and expanded once more to fill two thirds of the sky.

Stella felt her skin prickle under her protective scales. She was soaring in thin air. From *Paulus* One Alone shared with her, saw with her eyes and his senses as the aurora sent out a long streamer of reds and purples to lash and coil around Stella's smooth-scaled form. For a full second she was a gleaming mote in a sea of color.

The glowing fields of rainbow hues fell swiftly toward the surface, whipped away toward the north, and disappeared.

The rising moon was dim against the glowing sky.

CHAPTER ELEVEN

LaConius turned from the computer terminal and grinned. "I've double-checked. There's nothing about the aurora in Sparks or anywhere else."

"Great," John said.

"Auroras, most often called northern lights, are not uncommon," LaConius said, "but nowhere do they seem to be of the intensity that we saw just now. I think we've got something."

"I'm pleased for you, Cone," John said.

"For all of us," LaConius said.

Cecile heard the words, but she was in shock. LaConius of Tigian was not what he seemed to be. He was so attractive, so handsome. He seemed to be genuinely interested in the welfare of the others, but he was serious when he called Clear Thought that name— Lizard Face.

She could remember that LaConius had started teasing Clear Thought even before the expedition lifted off from Xanthos. He used the name, Lizard Face, as if he were being loving and funny, but he thought that Clear Thought was ugly, even subhuman.

She felt nauseous. LaConius had a mind like a small, furry animal. While he was talking to John, he looked at

her and she was shocked anew. His attentions, which she
had once welcomed, took on an entirely different coloration when she knew his true feeling for her. He thought
of her only with lust, and with a disdain for her as a non-
Tigian. He thought that of all the members of the expedition she was the lightweight.

She shifted uncomfortably as his eyes dropped. She
had to resist an urge to tug on her short skirt, felt
shamed by the normal display of her well-shaped, long,
graceful legs. In confusion she closed herself off. When
she poked her mind out again, somewhat like a reptile
sticking its head carefully out of a protective shell to
see if the danger was past, she felt a storm of thoughts,
a confusion of emotions as all of them came at her in
a solid wave of sensations. The weight of it stunned
her. She swayed on her feet.

"Close yourself, daughter," One Alone said to her.

"Yes," she whispered, desperately seeking privacy.
"I'm fine now."

"Glad to hear it," John said, "but who asked?"

He was looking at her with concern. His mind was
clean, fresh. He was just John, a seeker of beauty, sensitive. She flushed as, for the first time, she sensed that
he saw beauty in her.

"Stop, now," One Alone said. "Go to your cabin. We
must talk."

"In a minute," she said aloud. John looked at her
questioningly again.

She knew the wonderfully organized mind of Clear
Thought, the sweetness that was Stella. They had
beamed thoughts to her on previous occasions, but
never without asking her permission. This was some-

thing new and disturbing, an intimacy she neither sought nor wanted.

Martha. Calm, but suffering from menstrual cramp. Back to John. Pure, bright. He was thinking of the aurora, seeing it with the eyes of an artist.

But how long had LaConius been undressing her in his mind? It was written into the individual expedition contracts that personal relations would be limited, meaning specifically that there would be no sex lest such activity lead to jealousies and friction. LaConius was trying to think of a way to get around the restriction. He was looking at her as if she were a Tigian whore, a piece of merchandise that he could purchase on a whim. It was ugly.

She shied away and felt something new, a tenderness in John's mind when he looked at Martha. Martha was an open book, displaying her love for John as she returned his smile. It was rather beautiful. So much had passed between them in one glance. How had she, Cecile, failed to notice before that they were in love? Were they ignoring the contract stipulations? No. It was written in Martha's mind. Desire and innocence.

"Cecile," One Alone said, with vibrating force inside her skull.

Startled, she looked upward.

"You must not take advantage," One Alone said. "You must respect the right of privacy. This is a responsibility that is new to you, and it is vital that you observe the laws."

"The rules of privacy apply to Old Earthers and the partial telepaths of Belos II," she said, subvocalizing as she usually did when in communication with One Alone.

"And now to you, daughter."

"No." She spoke the word aloud. She felt her heart leap and she was frightened.

"I must speak to all," One Alone said. "Blank your mind, daughter." He gave her a hint as to how to accomplish that feat.

"As you say, LaConius," his voice said, coming to all of them, "you are onto something."

"Yeah, but what?" LaConius asked aloud.

"Be patient," One Alone said. "There is some data that I want to review. I request the presence of both Stella and Cecile aboard *Paulus* to aid me in this task."

"Aid you?" LaConius snorted. "A Far Seer asking for help?"

"It has happened before," One Alone said dryly.

Cecile spoke aloud. "We will all come up to *Paulus* together after we break camp."

"Have care," One Alone sent to her alone.

"Break camp?" LaConius asked. "We're not going anywhere until we have all the data we can gather on that aurora."

"That's why we're going to DW-3," Cecile said, with a certainty that drew astonished looks.

"If we go anywhere, I think we should try one of the planets on the outer fringe," John said. "The streamers put out by the aurora all pointed toward the core."

"We're not going anywhere," LaConius said.

Cecile turned to face LaConius. "DW-3," she said.

"Why?" Martha asked.

"Call it woman's intuition," Cecile said.

"DW-3 has heavy gases in the atmosphere," John said. "Are you thinking that because of the bad atmospheric conditions she might not have been as thoroughly examined as some other planets?"

"No," Cecile said. "That is not the reason."

"We have Clear Thought, who can explore in heavy atmosphere without armor," John said.

"You people are talking as if we're going somewhere," LaConius said, anger growing in his voice.

Cecile looked into the Tigian's eyes. Her green eyes narrowed as she sensed his musky, furry lust for her, and his almost unconscious contempt for her. She sent this thought into his mind, sent it with force. "You bastard, I am more than just a life-support for a vagina."

He stepped back as if he had been lashed in the face. She moved into his mind, twisted a tiny little thing in his head.

"No," One Alone thundered in her mind, but it was done.

"I am captain of this ship," LaConius said with mock sternness. "I say when we go and when we stay." He grinned. "And what I say is, we go. Load 'em up and move 'em out for DW-3. Who am I to stand in the way of a woman's intuition?"

"Daughter," One Alone said sadly, "do not attempt such a thing again."

Clear Thought was looking at LaConius in complete surprise. His eyes shifted to Cecile, and she knew that One Alone was in communication with him. She tried to hear, but the Old Earthers had been in control of their minds for millennia. Clear Thought looked away guiltily.

Cecile slept little that night. She spent the long hours exploring herself, for there was so much that was new. She helped dismantle the camp and as the two scouts rose toward *Paulus* she relaxed for the first time since she had stood under the full display of the aurora. Words formed in her mind.

"—slight alteration in brain wave patterns in the prefrontal area," One Alone was saying.

"I have not detected them," Stella said.

Cecile could only conclude that they had opened their minds to her voluntarily.

"The changes in your own brain wave patterns are much like those of the light-haired one," One Alone said, and that third person reference told Cecile that she was evesdropping.

"What are your conclusions?" Stella asked.

"I have none as yet. I'm concerned. The bright-hair does not know how to control her new abilities. She made a quick and effortless adjustment in the mind of LaConius."

Cecile's face burned with anger. "One Alone," she thought, "I must tell you that I hear what you are saying."

She felt their minds retreating in shock. Her anger faded. "Please," she said, "I didn't intend to intrude on your privacy. It just happened."

There was silence. She reached out, wanting to reassure them that she was sincere, to soothe their shock. She found Stella, she of the sweetness of mind, and to her surprise there was in Stella's pure being a sense of panic.

"Stella, please," she said, trying to ease Stella's travail.

"Cease at once," One Alone said sternly.

"I told you that I had no desire to offend you," Cecile said. She thought goodwill, even love. She felt

One Alone as she'd never felt him before. There was a stern kindness there, and worry.

"You must learn," One Alone said.

"She breached me," Stella said in wonder. "She did it quite easily. I closed to her and she came in without effort."

"I didn't mean to hurt you," Cecile said.

"I think you can understand Stella's agitation better when I tell you that you have done something that not even I could have done without help. Not even a Far Seer can enter the closed mind of a Power Giver against her will. I don't understand as yet how you can do it, but I know that you have acquired a talent, daughter, that can be used for harm or for good. It is vital to all of us, and to you, that you learn to use it wisely."

"Please help me," Cecile said.

"Of course we will," Stella said.

"Please withdraw, Stella," One alone said.

Cecile was alone with the Far Seer. The scout was nearing *Paulus.*

"First, we must determine the extent of your gift," One Alone said. "When I come close to you reach out as you did toward Stella. See if you can find my mind. If you do, you will feel something that is the mental equivalent of a hard shell. Do your best to enter that shell."

"Are you sure?"

"You have my permission," One Alone said.

She felt a new kind of silence, a loneliness that was dark and foreboding. She could feel the presence of the others, but she shut them out and searched for One

Alone. The scout was being inserted into its berth in a pod on the side of the *Paulus*.

She felt the closed dome of One Alone's mind. The shape was much like his head. She could see and feel him, his hairless, pointed dome, his eyeless face. She was still alone. She felt deserted. She needed his knowledge. She was frightened. She was exploring a new world and there was no one to guide her. She panicked. She screamed at One Alone with her mind. There was no answer. She flung herself at his bald dome and sank into a feeling of agony, fear, shock. She had a brief impression of overwhelming love, the love of the Far Seer for his Keeper, knew the feel of soft, hot flesh, fled from this ultimate invasion of privacy.

"I'm sorry," she said.

The Far Seer was a long time in answering. "You went deeper than I thought was possible."

"You love her so very much," Cecile said. "It's so beautiful."

"Yes. My relationship with my Dear Companion has always been something that only another Far Seer could comprehend, but you understood and empathized in seconds."

"She's pretty," Cecile said. "And so gentle."

"We must talk."

"Yes, please."

"For the moment we will keep all of this from the others."

"Is that fair for you Old Earthers to know and to keep it secret from John, LaConius, and Martha?"

Clear Thought's voice came to both of them as an intrusion. "One Alone, forgive me for entering without invitation. We felt a great force."

"Yes, it's all right," One Alone said. He quickly sent a mental impression of what Cecile had done.

Clear Thought expressed shock.

"He's gone," Cecile said, after Clear Thought had withdrawn. "May I please come to your cabin to see Dear Companion?"

"If you like, when we have finished talking. With some little instruction you will be able to store and withdraw information from her."

"I want to know more of the history of your people."

"Go to your cabin, please," One Alone said.

"Yes." She broke away from the others as quickly as possible.

"I'll be frank with you," One Alone sent to her as she closed the door to her cabin. "You have a power unlike that of anyone who has gone before. It is a fearsome thing. No Healer, no Power Giver, not even another Far Seer could have passed so easily through my privacy shield."

"What has happened to me?" Cecile asked.

"I think you know, at least subconsciously, the answer to that."

"It has to do with the aurora, doesn't it?"

"Yes, but don't ask me to explain it, not just yet. The only detectable change in you physically is an alteration in the activity of the cerebral cortex."

"Why do you say that I'm different from you and the other Old Earthers? Can't you do the things I'm doing?"

"I could not, as I have told you, break the privacy shield of another Far Seer. Do you know how you entered my mind?"

"No, not really. I just seemed to sink down through—"

"My bald, pointed dome," he said, without humor. "I was guarding the front door. You slipped in through the back door, through my subconscious mind. Do you realize the significance of that?"

"I think so. That's the inaccessible part of the mind, right?"

"Even I have to undergo hours of deep contemplation and self-hypnotism to access that area of my brain."

Cecile poured a glass of fruit nectar, sipped it.

"Will you submit to tests?" the Far Seer asked.

"Yes, of course."

"What do you know about the powers of a Far Seer?"

"That they are very impressive."

"I'm going to withdraw. When I am gone, close your mind. I will try to do what you did, to enter without permission. There will be no pain."

"I know," she said.

He was gone. Around her the ship made its little housekeeping sounds. She heard a relay click, felt a rush of cool air as the cooling system adjusted the temperature in her cabin. From far away a clang of metal was carried through the hull. She reached out. Clear Thought and LaConius were securing the hatches to the scout bays. She waited. Nothing. She checked her watch. Five minutes had passed. She drank her nectar and waited five more minutes, then said, "When are you going to start?"

"I started the second you closed," One Alone said.

"I didn't hear you."

One Alone sounded grim. "No, you very definitely did not. Can you read the others?"

Cecile let her mind touch each in turn. "Yes," she said.

"Where is the satellite of DW-13?"

"I don't know."

"Look." He showed her the scene, another world swimming in space, a large moon. "Now try."

"No, I can't feel such things."

For over an hour the Far Seer probed and tested. To his astonishment his assessments seemed to make her mental abilities stronger. At last there was only one more test.

"You know, daughter, that I have the ability to halt the involuntary functions of the brain. It is, quite effectively, the power of life and death. It has been used only a few times in our history. You have demonstrated a strength that is superior to mine in all other aspects. Will you allow me to give you this one last test?"

"You're going to try to kill me?"

"I want only to see if you can resist this ultimate use of mental force. The worst that will happen to you is that you might have some minor difficulty in breathing. I want you to resist my force, repel it if you can. If I can penetrate your defense, you will feel a small discomfort, then I'll stop."

She braced herself. She felt the rise of fear in her chest, a tension, a closing together, and then a fluttering of her heart. She fought and she felt immediate relief. She was disappointed. She felt as if she'd lost something valuable, for there had been, to that moment, a certain sense of security in knowing that One Alone, wise, kind, loving, was looking after her. She wanted to submit to him, and in doing so she began to die slowly. Her breathing was labored. Her heart was skipping. An elemental force rose up in her. Her survival instinct sent something screaming through her mind, a slashing, screaming ferocity that defied her even when she tried to stop it. She told herself that One Alone would not kill her, that he would stop, but there was terror and panic and anger and her lungs were heaving, taking in precious, life-giving air even as the slashing force continued to strike outward.

A voice was screaming in her mind and then was silent. She fell weakly into her chair and reached out for One Alone. She encountered a void, a cold blankness. One Alone was not breathing. She searched and felt a weak force beating at the edge of her mind, nothing more than a feeble flutter. She opened wide and knew that the faint beat of life was One Alone's dying brain.

"Come back," she said forcibly. "Come back now."

He breathed and his life-force leapt upward. "What have we done?" he asked.

Cecile searched and found that terrible coldness. They were in various positions. Stella and Martha were in their beds. LaConius and Clear Thought lay on the metal deck in the portside scout bay. John was slumped over the table in the galley.

"Help me, One Alone," Cecile begged, as she sent to Stella first and then, in a frenzy, for the precious seconds were passing, to the others, Laconius last.

Stella and Clear Thought sent their minds searching, quickly knew what had happened.

"It's over," One Alone said. "It's all right."

Cecile saw beyond his reassuring words, knew that he was not expressing his true feelings. He was numb with shock. He was astounded that there was a mind aboard *Paulus* that could overwhelm his and, in seconds, spread death through the entire ship. He knew that he had been dying and that she had brought him back from death.

"One Alone," Cecile whispered. "Help me. Help me, please."

"Yes, daughter," he said. "For a little while. Then it is we who will be coming to you for help."

"Are they all right? Is there damage?"

"They are all right," One Alone said. "As for me, I am learning humbleness. I confess that it is an odd feeling. I am accustomed to being the guide, the strong one. Now I am forced to adjust to being relegated to a secondary position."

"No," Cecile said.

"Be wise," One Alone said.

"Tell me how to keep my mind under control. You are the strong one. You are the conscience of your race. You are the guardian of life. Tell me how to behave so that never again will I endanger my friends."

"For the moment, rest," One Alone said. "We will work together, you, Stella, Clear Thought, and I, until you have control over this power of yours."

Cecile was very tired. She undressed, got into bed.

"May I?" Stella asked with her mind.

"Yes, please." She felt the soothing, sweet blanket of Stella's concern wash over her. She felt love and a great hope for the future.

CHAPTER TWELVE

Log of *Paulus*
Sector F-10 Tri-Chart Ref. F-10-1
Position R-3.87, V-11.34, H-30.10, L-5.71
Subject: Fourth planet DW Primary E.
Signed: LaConius of Tigian

United Planets Yacht *Paulus* arrived DW-3 Month 2, Day 18. Two scout survey of planet Days 19 and 20. Camp established Day 21.

Preliminary findings agree with those recorded by the Mallow Expedition, the last group to survey DW-3. Atmospheric pressure at surface 1.6 Xanthos standard. Carbon dioxide base. Noxious gas analysis attached. Oxygen content .23 Xanthos standard. Surface temperatures 198–204 F. dayside, 150–160 F. nightside.

Sealed hut camp on northern land mass 1.5 miles from Mallow dig at map site North B-74, 5.8 miles from slope of ancient ocean basin, .35 miles from cliffs and slopes of coastal range of low mountains.

Personal remarks: It was a day's work setting up those huts. I was impressed by Clear Thought. He can breathe in the atmospheric soup of this hellhole. He vents the poisons through his gills after extracting the traces of oxygen. He cut the work of setting up camp by at least half, since the rest of us were in armor.

I'm still wondering why I let that damned Cecile stampede me into coming to DW-3. I can't explain what came over me, but once the decision was made, there was no backing out because the others regained their enthusiasm. Morale was very low after the boredom and sameness of those fruitless digs on DW-19.

So we're here, and there's nothing to do but make the most of it. Clear Thought did a walk-around and reports rubble heaps that have not been dug. That's understandable, since all of the past explorers have had to work in bulky life-support gear.

Cecile is very optimistic, but not at all articulate in explaining why. I'm giving her enough rope so that she's the one who will look foolish if we fail. I let her pick the campsite. It's not far from the caves discovered by the Mallow Expedition. (See *Combined Expeditions to the Dead Worlds,* Vol. 5, pp. 598–623.) Mallow spent most of his time on this planet clearing the caves, but he found nothing of significance.

I admit that I am beginning to feel a bit desperate. So far we've accomplished nothing new except to observe the aurora on DW-19 and consume a few millions of my father's money. Money is not the main consideration, but the Iboni family expects return on investment. I will not go back with nothing more than recycled observations and some colorful pictures of a display in a planetary magnetic field.

CHAPTER THIRTEEN

Cecile was the first one ready. She left the sealed hut through the air lock and waited outside. LaConius, bulky in the space armor, had not yet donned his helmet. He leaned over a table, studying a map drawn by the Mallow Expedition. John was not in life-support gear. He had volunteered to perform guard duty. He would stay in the hut, ready to come to the rescue in a scout ship if the field party got into trouble. Clear Thought was not in armor, but he carried oxygen in a backpack.

Cecile was more at ease when she was alone. She had learned to isolate herself from the sometimes disturbing thoughts of the others and to accept the changes that had occurred in her. However, there never seemed to be enough time to explore her own mind and to examine the unbridgeable gulf that had opened up between her and the others.

As she waited, she found herself picturing the bodies that made up the sac system. She could not yet sense distant gravitational fields with One Alone's accuracy, but she could pinpoint the position of any world in the system at any given moment and she could feel the movement of DW-3's two moons. As she thought about the intricate, integrated dance of the planets and stars of the system, she could penetrate to the inner workings of a complicated celestial machine and not only predict but understand its workings.

All this was odd to her, for she had not been the best student of astromechanics at Xanthos University. It pleased her to be able to project complicated patterns and to predict the future positions of a given world within the system. Most amazingly, she could perform the functions of a sophisticated computer and roll the movements of the system backward in time. It was an interesting game. She often used it to help block out stray thoughts from the others.

The steaming heat of dayside set the suit coolers working. One by one the other members of the field party came out of the lock. The armor was the most sophisticated equipment that money could buy, but it was like wading through water to move about in it. The murky air was lit only dimly by filtered sunlight.

"Communicators open at all times," LaConius reminded them. "Visual contact except for Clear Thought and Stella."

Cecile squinted to see a few yards ahead. Eyes were, after all, inferior instruments. She saw barren earth, a rubble heap. Condensation of the dense atmosphere formed a light coating of dull crystals on the rocks. It was all dead. It was all devastation, but she could sense, dimly, a world that had once been vibrant with life.

Clear Thought scouted the way. Stella soared once to get a feel for the planet's fields. LaConius reminded them that the outing was nothing more than a scouting exploration, that they were to stay together.

When Cecile first realized that she knew exactly what lay ahead, she was startled. She stopped and let John move past her. To her left was a passageway carved into the solid rock of the hill. She heard the chatter of her friends as if from a great distance.

"Don't fall too far behind," John said to her via the communicators.

There were piles of rubble everywhere. A wind moved the heavy atmosphere sluggishly. Although the coolers were working perfectly, it was stuffy in the armor. The recycled air tasted stale. Cecile halted again, let the others move ahead and fade into the murk. She turned and walked directly toward the cliffs.

"I am with you, daughter." For a moment she had left herself open so that One Alone's thoughts came to her. Her first reaction was irritation, but that faded quickly as she became more widely separated from the party.

"Yes," she said. "Stay with me, please."

"Perhaps it would be best if you rejoined the others."

"No, but I confess that I'm scared."

She could see One Alone. He sat in a great chair in his quarters aboard *Paulus*. She was familiar now with his bald, pointed, eyeless dome. His hands were lying on the table in front of him. His stateroom was almost bare. In the bedchamber Dear Companion slept.

"Cecile?" It was LaConius on the communicator. "Where in hell are you?"

"You should answer," One Alone said, after a long silence.

She spoke into the communicator. "I'm moving directly toward the base of the cliff which is a few hundred feet to the west of your line of travel," she said.

"I told you to stay in visual contact," LaConius said angrily. "Get back in line. We'll wait for you."

"Go ahead," Cecile said.

"Damn it," LaConius said. "We're going to go into the caves."

"All right," Cecile said. "Go ahead. I'll catch up later."

"I have you in view, Cecile," Stella said.

Cecile looked up. She could not see the soaring Power Giver in the murk.

"Stella, will you please bring that silly twit to us?" LaConius asked.

"No, Stella," Cecile said sharply.

"Daughter," One Alone said, "do you give the orders now?"

Clear Thought said, "I'll go stay with Cecile until she joins us."

"All right," LaConius said. "I don't care what the hell you do."

Cecile moved as swiftly as possible in the bulky armor. The cliff towered over her. For a moment she was puzzled, for there seemed to be only vertical planes of stone, but then she moved to her left, circled a huge fallen boulder, wound her way to the face of the cliff and there was the entrance to a cave that Mallow had worked. He had labeled it a secondary site. LaConius and the others were planning to enter the larger caverns a half mile or so farther on.

Cecile turned off her communicator. The suit's power system hummed faintly. She could hear her own breathing, sense the pounding of her heart. She was in a smoothly excavated tunnel, walking on an accumulation of dust. The tunnel took two right angle turns. She was in total blackness illuminated only by the light mounted on her helmet. Uncountable tons of rock were over her, around her. The bulk of a mountain pressed down on her, but she brushed aside her uneasiness and moved forward. She no longer questioned the obvious fact that she was being guided to a definite destination. The tunnel made another sharp turn.

"What is it you seek?" One Alone asked her.

"I can't answer that," she said.

The smoothly cut tunnel arrowed directly into the mass of the mountain. At one point a rockfall blocked Cecile's progress. She hesitated only a moment before crawling over the top of the fall on her stomach.

Clear Thought was trying to contact her. She blocked him and did not answer. The burden of rock atop her made her imagine being trapped on her stomach with rubble holding her down, but she forced herself to move on. She told herself that if she were caught by a cave-in One Alone would guide the others to her. The disassembler could cut quickly through any cave-in.

In the clear again, with only accumulated dust on the floor of the tunnel, Cecile ran heavily, panting with her efforts. She came to a halt when she sensed space around her. Her helmet light showed walls behind her but did not reach the other side of what she felt to be a large, domed chamber. She followed the wall to the left and when she turned her head, the beam of light was eaten by the murk of the atmosphere.

Cecile made no attempt to estimate distance. The walls curved for a time, then flattened. The light showed the wall surface to be smooth and unmarked. She felt keen disappointment and didn't understand why. She had been drawn to the spot. That was the only allowable conclusion, for she no longer felt the urge to move forward.

She was alone under a mountain. She felt the skin crawl at the nape of her neck. For a moment she was a young, rather small girl in a dark place. She fought the urge to call for Clear Thought, or to turn and run toward the dim light of the outdoors.

"I am with you," One Alone said reassuringly.

"I feel something," she said.

"May I share?"

"Yes. Can you feel it?"

"Something," One Alone said. "Not strong."

She faced the blank, smooth rock wall. The beam of her light reflected glaringly.

"It is time for you to rejoin the others," One Alone said.

"Not yet."

There was *something*. She felt it. It hovered just beyond the limits of her awareness. She touched the wall with her gloved hand. The sense of touch built into the armor told her that the rock was smooth. It had a texture like marble, and she concentrated on the smoothness.

"The others are concerned about you," One Alone said. "Clear Thought is moving toward the entrance."

She sighed, turned on the communicator. "LaConius, do you read?"

"I do," LaConius said. "Where are you?"

"I'm in the easternmost cave, one of those that Mallow called secondary. I'm fine. Don't worry."

"Anything in there?" LaConius asked.

"Dust," Cecile said.

"I am coming in," Clear Thought said.

"Since you're so damned hardheaded," LaConius said, "we'll come in, too. Stay put until we get there."

"There is a rockfall halfway in," she said. "You have to crawl over the top of it."

It would be some time before they reached her. Cecile stared at the blank wall, rubbed it with her gloved hand, and let her thoughts play over it. A sense of urgency was building in her, but she was reluctant to—for a better term—externalize her mind. The last time she had gone out of herself she had spread death throughout the *Paulus*.

She felt like screaming in frustration. Something wonderful was almost within her grasp, waiting for her. She had only to find the proper key. She let her mind go out tentatively, felt it penetrate into the solid stone, thinking that perhaps there was, behind the smooth wall, a hidden cavern. There was nothing. She probed the cavern, knew bare stone walls, open space, the deep coating of dust on the cavern floor. But she was near, so near *something*.

Moving away from the spot near the smooth wall, Cecile walked into the open space of the chamber and almost immediately felt an inexplicable tug that led her back to the same position by the wall. Frustrated, she let her mind go blank and felt the slow, ponderous dance of the astral bodies of the sac system.

"Why do I keep thinking of that?" she asked. "What do the motions of the stars and the planets have to do with the way I feel."

"There is an answer somewhere," One Alone said.

She reviewed the reports of the Mallow Expedition. One of her new talents was to be able to summon up anything she had ever read. The pages of the Mallow report flashed across her awareness in an instant.

Mallow had noted an accumulation of fine dust piled against the wall of the cavern. He had removed the dust in some areas.

Why was she thinking about the dust? Mallow had excavated some, but it covered the floor, was a soft cushion underfoot. Why was it important?

She concentrated hard, trying to see the chamber as it was when Mallow first opened it. She succeeded. Before Mallow's excavations there had been large piles of dust just below the walls of the chamber. She closed her eyes and asked, *why*? Why were there piles of dust before Mallow cleared them?

"I think you need to open your eyes and look around you," One Alone said.

She gasped in surprise. There were banks of dust, piles of dust against the wall. She reached out to touch them. What she saw was real, and it had not been there when she closed her eyes.

"One Alone, what is happening?" she asked.

"I want you to be very careful," One Alone said. "We are dealing with forces that I don't understand."

"I understand one thing," she said. "I'm scared."

"Yes," One Alone said. "I sense danger. I can't define it, but I suggest that you do nothing more. Do nothing until we can do some controlled testing."

Suddenly her fear drained from her. "It is the dust," she said.

"Wait," One Alone said. "At least wait until Clear Thought is with you."

"The dust came from the wall," Cecile said. "It was a part of the wall."

She externalized and examined individual, tiny grains of dust. She let her mind sink down into the banks of it, searching, probing, and the solution came to her with blinding clarity. She saw the sac system dancing in eternal motion. She rolled the image backward in time, faster, faster, until the motion was so swift that she couldn't follow it. She felt joy, for at her feet the banks of dust stirred, lifted, flowed, blocked the beam of her light. When the visibility cleared, she cried out in wonder.

Her light was playing over shapes and forms and brilliant colors.

The work was in bas-relief, and it was huge. It extended upward toward the ceiling, which was lost in the murkiness of the air. She backed away, breathing fast. Her light made circles on the wall. It illuminated only relatively small areas of the huge work of art. She was desperate to see all of it, to have the whole of it in her consciousness.

Light, she thought. I have to have light.

She felt a quick dizziness and then the chamber glowed as if each molecule of the dense and poisoned air had a light source of its own. She blinked at the sudden brightness, blinded. Willing her pupils to contract, Cecile squinted upward to catch the tableau on the wall in all its glory.

There was a simple beauty in the work that made her eyes mist. She smiled. Colors seemed to leap out from the wall, but the full effect of the work was dimmed by the clouded air.

Clear Thought, leading the way into the cave, was pushed backward by a sudden gust of wind coming from the interior. Dust roiled and there was a sucking sound and the murk that had obscured his view was gone.

"What was that?" LaConius asked. He and the others were just beyond the first bend of the tunnel, a short distance behind Clear Thought.

The suit servomechanisms clicked and purred as adjustments were made to the new environment, which was, Clear Thought realized quickly, a hard vacuum. He sent a quick query to One Alone. He wasn't sure whether to be relieved or frightened when One Alone informed him that the change had been effected by Cecile. He filled his lungs with oxygen from his backpack and ran forward, rapidly outdistancing the others.

Stella lifted to soar down the tunnel after Clear Thought. LaConius continued to demand to be told what had happened.

The members of the party arrived in the main chamber one by one. After their first reaction, which was to halt as if frozen, their emotions varied. Clear Thought and Stella, warned in advance by One Alone as to what to expect, were still very much affected.

Stella wept, for to see the work of art on the wall of the cavern brought home to her the extent of the loss when twenty worlds were destroyed. Clear Thought, too, was awed by his first full realization of the implications of the disaster. Together with Stella he mourned the passing of the beings who were pictured in the carvings on the wall.

LaConius felt a surge of triumph. The expedition was not only a success, it would be a sensation. By God, he told himself, this will show those old bastards at the university who were against my mounting another expedition to the Dead Worlds.

Martha's first thought, on seeing the work, was of John. What a pity it was that he was not with them to be among the first to discover such a beautiful piece of art. John, the artist among them, would be the last to see.

Finally, there was another common reaction. They stood in silence, heads back, looking up at the wall. Each knew his own thoughts, but they were mixed with wonder, and no little fear.

The bas-relief extended for three hundred feet along the wall and reached to the ceiling, two hundred feet above them. For all its majesty it was tastefully simple; and so skillfully executed that it seemed to live.

It was only later that any of them would wonder about the source of the strong, even light which seemed to be designed to show shadows where they were needed and to highlight textures realistically.

"If they move," Martha said, "don't get between me and the way out."

Each of them understood, for the figures seemed prepared to step down from the wall and stride about the chamber.

There were, in spite of the heroic size of the sculpture, only two figures. One was male, the other female. The female's stomach bulged with life. They were very definitely humanoid, if, indeed, the definition of the word could be enhanced to cover such beauty of face and form.

LaConius stared at the female. In spite of her obvious pregnancy, she was the most sensuous image he'd ever seen. Her pointed breasts were artfully exposed by the design of her gaily colored costume. Her eyes were huge, almond shaped, tilted. Her lips were full.

Clear Thought was admiring the male, for his long, muscular legs had been designed to cover ground tirelessly. The male's clothing could have been designed for athletic activity. A belted tunic ended at his upper thigh.

"His face is so kind," Stella said. "And she is so gentle. They love each other very much."

Only Cecile noticed that Stella spoke of the depicted pair in the present tense. She thought, I know you. She blocked out the others, including One Alone. I know you, and you are truly beautiful, both of you.

It was not yet time—they were all still in the midst of exhilaration—to wonder how the Mallow Expedition could have overlooked such a treasure. Each of them was lost in his own thoughts.

It was Martha who broke the awed silence. "He's holding a star in his hand."

"John will want to find out how the artist made the star glow," Stella said, for the object in the hand of the male contained some of the brightness of a sun.

"They're standing in front of a model of the sac system," LaConius said.

"There is an interesting symbolism in the stance of the male," Clear Thought said. "That band of stars he's straddling is the Milky Way Galaxy."

"He's telling us that the galaxy is his," Martha said.

"The star in his hand is a symbol of power," Stella said. "He controls the galaxy, and in the background—" She pointed. "Aren't those other galaxies?"

"What is the light source?" Clear Thought asked One Alone privately.

"The light source is Cecile," One Alone said.

Clear Thought looked musingly at the bright-haired girl.

LaConius called John, back at camp, and told him to bring a light recorder as quickly as possible. John landed a scout near the tunnel's entrance within minutes and was soon in the chamber, his eyes filling with his emotion as he stood, stricken by the pure beauty.

"Get on with it," LaConius said. "I want thousands of feet of pictures. I want to know why Mallow didn't report this. I want to know the age of that picture. I want to know what tools were used to carve it and the chemical makeup of the colors." He paused, turning toward Cecile. She had been standing almost motionless for a half hour.

"What I want to know most, Cecile, is how you knew where to go and why the atmosphere was evacuated as we came in?"

Cecile seemed not to hear.

LaConius was too elated to be bothered. "We're going to knock them on their backsides back in the U.P.," he said.

One Alone spoke to all of them. "All work will be postponed," he said. "The entire company will return to camp immediately and board *Paulus* with all haste."

"You've got to be kidding," LaConius said.

"I remind you, LaConius of Tigian," One Alone said solemnly. "It is written into the charter of this expedition that I am guardian against dangers not detectable by others. In such an event, which I now declare, my word is law."

"Danger?" Martha asked, looking around nervously.

"Don't do this to me," LaConius begged. "Not just when we're getting somewhere. There's work to be done, One Alone. There are questions to be answered. Where is the light coming from, for example?"

"That will be explained during our conference aboard ship," One Alone said.

"You know the source of the light?" LaConius asked.

"I know, and it is time you know, also," One Alone said. "Do you agree, daughter?"

Cecile turned reluctantly away from her study of the bas-relief. "I suppose so," she said.

CHAPTER FOURTEEN

The original settlement of Selbelle III had been termed by some historians an exercise in elitism. The colonists were selected for artistic talent coupled with achievements in scientific fields. Applicants were examined down to and including the DNA level and only those with genes untainted by hereditary faults were chosen.

The grand experiment had proven to be successful. Thousands of years after the first aristocracy of a new world took up residence on the shores of a balmy, tropical sea, Selbelle III continued to be the artistic center of the United Planets Confederation. Its citizens enjoyed the highest standard of living known to man.

John was a true Selbellian. First and foremost, he was an artist. His work, young as he was, had been displayed not only on his home planet but on a dozen other worlds, including sophisticated Xanthos. In addition to his artistic ability, he had taken a degree in cultural studies at the university. He was a confident young man who was assured of a splendid future. The first effect the bas-relief in the cave had on John was to strike a severe blow at his self-confidence, for the work made him feel like a clumsy apprentice. Moreover, since the people of Selbelle III were more aware of personal appearance than most, he was intimidated by the perfection of the male and the radiant beauty of the woman. His body features were the same as those pictured on the wall, but the more he studied the light recordings the more he was aware of his imperfections.

On Selbelle III a cosmetic surgeon with a good bed-side manner became wealthy soon after his graduation from medical school, but not even corrective surgery could bring a human face to the ideal pictured in the bas-relief. No regime of diet and exercise could ever produce so perfect a body.

To John's trained eye there were subtle differences in bone structure to account for the grace displayed by the two figures. U.P. man, in spite of aeons of striving, had not yet overcome the human tendency to suffer from the lower back problems that were inherent in a creature whose ancestors went about on all fours. The human spine had evolved—or been designed—to be a horizontal bridge, not a vertical pillar. That weakness of design was not evident in the portraits of the former inhabitants of DW-3. Backs were straight and the change made for aesthetic beauty in the line of hips and thighs.

For the first time in his life John found himself to be on the short side of a comparison. On his home world there was an insect called the flame-winged moth, which went through an extra stage after chrysalis. The first winged stage of the moth was spectacular, but the adult stage, the second chrysalis, was exquisite, altering the insect into the most magnificent butterfly in the U.P. Sector. When he compared himself with the male in the bas-relief, John was only the first stage, the DW-3 male the second winged stage of the flame-winged moth. The difference was that John had no hope of every maturing into perfection.

As many men had discovered before him, there is pain in being able to recognize beauty without being able to attain it. To console himself, he reasoned that the portraits were abstractions, idealizations of reality, with the unattainable beauty being nothing more than an artistic wish. Nothing could be so perfect.

There was an arrogance in the male who stood astride a galaxy, handling a star as if it were a toy. Surely he did not represent reality, not even a dead and past actuality.

John was both saddened by the loss of loveliness and encouraged by the comfort of his speculations. He let himself enjoy the work, but soon disturbing thoughts returned. It elevated him to believe that such flawlessness could have lived, but the perfection daunted him. In the end he accepted it, because the artist in him could not rationalize away an ideal once that ideal was discovered.

On another, more practical plane, the work of art created more questions than answers. People who stood astride a galaxy would, by extension, have the power to destroy worlds. Behind perfection had there been rot and decay? Could such beings have the moral abandon to do terrible deeds? If one man could have control of a galaxy, were there others who wielded equal power, thus setting the stage for a terminal war? Had the inhabitants of the Dead World attained such perfection that they committed the ancient sin of man, pride, and thus brought down the wrath of some jealous god? Could one rule out natural catastrophe of a kind not comprehensible to mere humans? Had there been an invasion from the depths of space?

All these questions and more were discussed aboard the *Paulus*. One Alone made one of his rare physical appearances among them. Looking at the Far Seer gave John more food for thought. One Alone could not, by any stretch of the imagination, be called attractive, but in many ways he was superior to the Old Ones, to the original form of Homo Sapiens. Was, then, physical beauty so important?

LaConius was moody. He sensed none of the danger about which One Alone had warned. His tenseness was mirrored in the others, for they were all young and they were stimulated by the discovery in the cavern, eager to get back to the surface of DW-3. At first, because of their agitation, the meeting was disorganized, with several people trying to talk at once.

"How in the hell did Mallow miss the pictures?" LaConius yelled, raising his voice to be heard.

"Because the pictures were not there when Mallow was on the planet," One Alone said.

There was a burst of questions. The Far Seer lifted his hands for silence. "If you'll listen, I can explain."

"All right," LaConius said sullenly. "I'm listening."

"The sculpture was destroyed along with everything else when the planet died," One Alone said. "It was reduced to dust. If you'll check the pictures in Mallow's accounts, you'll see that banks of dust lay against the walls in all of the caverns."

"Then how—" LaConius began. He sank back in his chair. "All right. I'm listening."

"Cecile reassembled the pictures from the dust," One Alone said.

"No," Martha said quickly. "I can't accept that. I don't believe in magic."

"It is not magic," One Alone said. "Cecile applied a very real power."

"Hell," LaConius said. "Mallow cleared away the dust from the caverns. How could she reassemble something which was scattered all over the globe by winds?"

"When we left the cave," Clear Thought said, "I noticed that the dumps where Mallow discarded the material he had excavated from the caves had been disturbed. Some of the dust and rubble had been removed. Small amounts, true, but there had been a definite disturbance in the mounds."

"And there was a small dust storm in the tunnel," Stella said.

"We know something happened," LaConius said. "Are you telling us, One Alone, that Cecile has the ability to re-create something that once existed on this world?"

"Yes," One Alone said.

"Given that she has somehow become able to do magic," Martha said, "how do we know, if she did assemble that picture, that it wasn't an original creation of her own?"

"No," Cecile said.

"Some of your questions will not be answered at this moment," One Alone said. "I would like to take a few moments to address the possible source of Cecile's new and 'magical' abilities. As you know, I have been making a detailed study of the movements of the bodies of the sac system. I have included in my calculations every cosmic body, some of which are too tiny to be seen without optical instruments."

"What's that got to do with—"

One Alone interrupted LaConius. "I have discovered that there is a cycle of celestial interaction that repeats itself. This conclusion is confirmed by the bas-relief. If you'll study the star map behind and around the figures you'll see that each body is almost exactly in the positions they occupy at the present moment. If we accept the estimates of the time that has passed since the destruction of these worlds, we must assume that in the star map in the cavern we are seeing the sac as it was seventy-five-thousand years ago."

"Look, let's discuss the important thing about all this," Martha said, breaking in. "Let's talk about what has happened to Cecile. I can accept the fact that you Old Earthers are different. I find it a little hard to conceive of Cecile as superwoman."

One Alone sensed fear in Martha. "There is nothing evil about using the power of the mind, if that power is used properly. There has been much speculation that the entire race is evolving toward the possession of greater mental powers."

"But over geological time, not instantly, as in Cecile's case," John said.

"Is there an assumption that can be made from that?" One Alone asked.

"Good question," John said, thinking of the lusty male image in the cavern. "If it can happen to Cecile, it can happen to all of us."

"My question was intended to mean a bit more than that," One Alone said. "Could such abilities have been developed suddenly in an entire race?"

"I get your point," Stella said. "That would explain why civilization sprang up so swiftly on the sac planets."

"But do we assume that the powers developed into ultimate destruction?" LaConius asked.

"Cecile created light in the cavern," Clear Thought said. "That's pretty impressive."

"It explains why no one has determined a source of power," Stella said. "Cecile wouldn't need electricity, therefore there was no need for nuclear generating plants or solar generators. They used fossil fuel for a brief period and then abandoned even that because each of them could create his own power."

John noticed that Cecile had chosen to sit all the way across the lounge from the rest of them. She was no longer the laughing, happy, all too human girl. Now she was a superbeing who could create light without a power source. In one instant she had outdated the entire body of scientific knowledge.

"There is no need for us to get too excited," LaConius said. "We're into something new, but facing a new situation is not a unique event. It's happened before, and man has always triumphed."

"When he wasn't smushed like a bug," John said.

"We can handle this situation if we stick together," LaConius said, "and come out of it with the galaxy by the tail."

"You wouldn't look good standing on top of the Milky Way," Martha said.

"I think one of the first things we have to determine," LaConius said, "is what brought about the change in Cecile. I could use a few magic tricks myself. Think about it. If we all could do what Cecile did in the cavern, we could reconstruct this whole planet. We'd have the answers once and for all."

"It's very simple," Martha said. "Cecile was the only one who was exposed to the aurora."

LaConius was thoughtful for a moment. John shifted uneasily in his chair.

"All right," LaConius said. "We'll go back to DW-19 and take an aurora bath."

"I cannot agree to that course of action without further study," One Alone said.

LaConius scowled. "Then start your studies, cone-head," he said. "You, Cecile, since you can work magic, get to work at it."

"We must proceed with great caution," One Alone said. "It is our duty to inquire, but not even Cecile is aware of the extent of her abilities. We have no idea what might happen through no fault of hers from some misapplication of a power she doesn't even know she has."

LaConius leapt to his feet, his face dark. "Work with her, then," he said, "but I'm going to get on with it. I'm going planet-side. Anyone with me?"

Cecile stood. There was something about her that riveted their attention. "You have been talking about me as if I were not here," she said evenly, "as if I am just some sort of new instrument designed for your use."

"Getting sensitive, superwoman?" LaConius asked.

"I'm tired," Cecile said. "I'm going to sleep."

One Alone spoke to Cecile in private. "While the events are fresh in your mind, will you enter your thoughts and feelings into the mind of my Keeper before you sleep?"

"If you wish," Cecile said, beginning the chore as she walked out of the lounge.

John, left alone with Martha, mused over his light recorder pictures. Martha poured glasses of wine and they looked at the pictures together.

"I could restore Terra II to her original beauty," Martha said. "I could put fertility back into the soil, cleanse the waters, make the air pure."

"And make the planet attractive enough to bring in a billion settlers?" John asked.

"If I had the power to remake the planet, I'd have the power to keep them out," she said. She swallowed hard. Her face flushed. "Listen to me. I'm not like that. I'm not a selfish monster."

"I know," John said, taking her hand.

"I don't even have Cecile's power and already I'm dreaming of using it against my fellow man."

John laughed. "I think you'd do the right thing," he said.

"What about you?"

"Power corrupts," he said, laughing, "and here's one fellow who is ready and willing to be corrupted."

"Even you? You've been thinking about it?"

"Guilty," he said. "I have dreamed of creating something even more beautiful than that damned bas-relief in the cave." He made a grand gesture. "John of Selbelle III, foremost artist of the galaxy." He patted her hand. "You see, I would be selfish, too."

"Is it selfish to want to be the best in your field?"

"No, I guess not, not if you compete fairly for it."

"There is that," she said.

"Man is a competitor. He began by fighting other animals for living space on Old Earth. He competes against nature, against time and distance in space, against himself. That's why we have human achievement. If I were given an unfair advantage by having the aurora make some magical little alteration in my brain, I'm not sure I'd enjoy being the best. I might feel that, after all, I, John of Selbelle III, was not responsible for the work, that it was the result of trickery."

"You could get greedy, couldn't you?" Martha asked. "If you could say a magic word and be the best artist, why not be the best musician, the most learned person in the galaxy, the prettiest."

"I think we're jumping to conclusions that might not be justified," John said. "After all, all Cecile has done is manipulate inert matter."

"She made light."

"It scares the hell out of me," John said, grinning. "And I don't like what it's done to her so far. She was always the life of the party. Now she's glum and serious."

"Maybe it's just the shock of it all," Martha said. "Having the power of life and death is enough to make you serious and glum."

"Life and death?"

"Remember the day we both fainted?"

"Yes."

"Have you ever passed out before?" she asked.

"Never."

"I've been thinking about that. I had a talk with Clear Thought last night. He wouldn't answer my questions directly, but he's not a good liar, as you know. His evasions and lack of answers made me feel that Cecile had something to do with what happened to us. I got Clear Thought to admit that he was unconscious, too. That's pretty scary, all of us passing out at the same time, just when Cecile is beginning to experiment with her magic."

John walked to the closed viewport, opened it. The world called DW-3 swam just beyond arm's length, it seemed, outside the port. He turned to look at Martha. "I can't believe she'd deliberately hurt us."

"One Alone hinted just now that she might do harm without intending it. Maybe she didn't realize what she was doing. Maybe she was just trying her wings."

"I hope you're wrong," John said.

"John, I want to go to DW-19. I want to stand outside in the aurora. Cecile's gone all odd. What would happen if someone made her angry?"

John brooded. He turned back to the port and watched the slow swirl of an atmospheric storm on the world below *Paulus*. He couldn't believe that Cecile was a source of danger to anyone, but he was uneasy. He thought about a world of people like Cecile, billions of beings with incalculable mental powers. As Martha said, what if someone made someone angry?

Stella had accompanied Clear Thought to his cabin. She sat with her long, scaled legs crossed. Clear Thought sprawled in the bed, hands under his large head. They had been close since undergraduate days at the university. Both knew that if they should color, should feel Nature's call to breed at the same time they would merge. The closeness between them would then coalesce into an attachment which would last past the one mating season decreed for them.

Stella's mind was open. She was thinking of romance. He gave her his regard in return. After a slow and pleasant time of dreaming together she sent him a direct thought.

"With the ability to reassemble past destruction we could uncover all of the secrets of the Old Ones. We could discover the true history of Old Earth, and of ourselves."

"There would be no more need, anywhere," Clear Thought said.

"We could open the galaxy. We could travel through intergalactic space."

"Mentally powered space travel," he said. "We'd do away forever with the limitation of the blink drive."

They considered the possibilities. The blink generator allowed a ship to travel through infinite space with no passage of time, but subspace travel was possible only in a straight line from one known point to another. When traveling in uncharted areas a ship could blink only to points within optical observation. The galaxy was large. The universe infinitely larger. Exploration consisted of a series of very short blinks interspersed with optical observation, the charging of the generators, movement in real space at speeds that obeyed the laws of relativity. If one could send a mental probe through parsecs of distance and follow it with a starship, it would be possible to explore the galaxy in a man's lifetime.

"One Alone detected change in my brain waves," Stella said, "but I developed no new abilities."

"Are you sure?" Clear Thought asked.

"There may be a very small increase in accuracy in the measurement of magnetic fields," she said. "But none of Cecile's magic."

"Your scales blocked the effect of the aurora."

"Or its effects are random," she said, "producing different results with different people."

"One Alone thinks that she is potentially dangerous," Clear Thought mused.

"The Old Ones do not have our total reverence for life."

Clear Thought knew that he would not hesitate to give unlimited mental power to Stella, or to any other Power Giver. The same was true for other members of his race. Old Earthers didn't have the craving for material things, and they lacked the hunger for power that often motivated the Old Ones. Old Earthers valued life above all. Life was the one irreplaceable gift that could be bestowed by Nature on an individual or a world, and it was sacred. In the hands of any Old Earther a gift like Cecile's would be used wisely.

However, it might be desirable to alter Nature's plan slightly. He shared with Stella, and felt a returned warmth when he dreamed of allowing more than one mating per lifetime for Power Givers and Healers. That did not seem unreasonable to either of them. The galaxy, unlike Old Earth, was capable of supporting a larger population of Old Earthers.

"If I had unlimited power," he mused, sharing with her, "I might allow myself the gift of Rack the Healer, known as the New One, because he had the ability to heal the cells of others as he could heal his own body."

Stella agreed that would be an unselfish change in Nature's plan, a change beneficial to all. "But," she said, "we are better adapted to live in a sometimes cruel universe than the soft Old Ones. If we bore young as easily and as often as they, would there be enough good planets to house us, or would we be relegated to the marginal worlds?"

"Would it be too destructive of Nature's plan to allow longer life spans?"

* * *

Cecile awoke to find One Alone waiting outside the portal of her mind. She allowed linkage and was patient as he probed and questioned. He quickly admitted that measuring the limits of her power was beyond his capacity.

"We know that the phenomenon is linked to the aurora," he said. "Help me, please."

Together they formed a model of the sac system and began to manipulate it. Swiftly they spun the whole backward in time, combining One Alone's ability to see distant bodies with Cecile's strength. She seemed to know instinctively the position of each body in the system at any given time. The ages rolled away. They backed time into a corner and began to tear away at it to uncover its secrets. The microcosmos which they created with the unity of their minds obeyed the laws of physics, acted and reacted with its surroundings and its individual members. Now and then, when interesting fields were created by positioning and interlaced gravitational and magnetic values, One Alone would freeze movement and make precise measurements.

They spun the model backward in time, past the landing of the spacers on Terra II, past the destruction of Earth. At a point 75,000 years in the past, in that microsystem created into solidity in the entity of their joined minds, the aurora swept upward from the northern polar regions of DW-19 and reached outward greedily into empty space. They saw it first as they went backward in time, and then forward. In the beginning the lights were feeble. In the end they swelled to enclose the planet and reach outward. At the crisis moment the force was not created by the magnetic field of DW-19 alone. It was a combination of fields from every large body in the sac, an interacting and interlaced complexity that colored the entire sac with a rainbow that exploded into blood red and then was gone.

One Alone froze that moment in time. They examined it and were astonished by its beauty.

"That's going to happen again," Cecile said.

"The cycle repeats itself," One Alone agreed, "over a 75,000 year period."

"So we've seen only the beginning of it," she whispered.

"There was life on at least one planet when it last happened," he said.

"What happens when the sky turns to flame?" she asked.

"The destruction," he said.

"Not from the aurora alone."

"No? What do you feel?"

"A confusion of fields, a chaos of influences, but that did not cause the destruction."

"The aurora changed them as you have been changed," One Alone said.

She shivered. "They built their civilizations, not knowing at first the extent of their powers. It happened so swiftly."

"And then they were dead," One Alone said.

"It won't happen again," she said, in answer to an unvoiced concern.

"I think you can learn to control yourself," he said. "But the fires will dance on all planets in this system, growing ever more intense. Your exposure, compared to what is to come, was a minor one. What happens to you, to all of us, in a full auroral storm?"

"We must stay," she whispered. Her green eyes were wide, and her face was pale.

"I fear so, daughter," he said.

"I'm so tired," she said.

"Sleep, then."

One Alone closed himself away and recorded his thoughts into the storage cells of his Keeper. His was a heavy burden. He was responsible for the lives of eight individuals, counting himself and Dear Companion. He had the legal authority, given in the charter of the expedition, to order departure from the sac. But never had a Far Seer—never had any man—had a greater opportunity.

It was a moral dilemma that kept him awake. If he forced the group to leave to avoid exposure to the coming auroral storms, he would have one changeling to study. It did not enter into his consideration that if he left before the storms he would remain inferior in power to Cecile. Far Seers had no ego. Far Seers were selfless.

By forcing the group to leave, he would be taking back into the populated areas of the U.P. a force, in the form of Cecile, which would have no counterpart. The force could be used for good, or for evil. Should he stay and risk the creation of other forces even more powerful than Cecile? Should he gamble that he would be affected by the aurora in proportion to his present mental abilities and, thus, become the prime power among superpowers? Given at least equal ability by the effects of the aurora he would be able to control the others.

The most basic question was: Would Nature's plan be irrevocably damaged by the introduction of superhumans into society? If so, then it was already too late, for Cecile was, and would be.

He would sleep on it. Dear Companion was awake and mewling for her nourishment. She was in need of sanitary attention, as well. He did his chores. She cooed in pleasure at being clean and dry and attacked her nourishment tube eagerly. To him, caring for her was a pure and simple joy. It was not just duty, it was bliss. How wrong were the Old Ones when they called Far Seers eternal baby-sitters.

Still, a Keeper was like Old One infants in helplessness and mentality, unlike them in the unused capacity of their large brains wherein was stored history, tradition, myth, scientific knowledge, and the random thoughts of their Far Seers. It was the team of Far Seer and Keeper who preserved knowledge in a society that developed no technology, had no written language, computed in mind pictures without mathematical symbols. Before the Reunification, Far Seers envisioned years only as complete circles, based on the orbit of the Earth around the sun, counted only by showing pictures of the objects to be assessed. Such feats would have been impossible without the brains of the Keepers.

In the solitary world of a Far Seer, isolated from the other forms of his race by relative immobility, by his lack of eyes and ears, there was but one brightness, his Keeper. He took comfort and pleasure from her. Unlike Power Givers and Healers, he was not limited to one period of sexual pleasure in a lifetime, but his frequent mergings—joyous for both him and for the Keeper— were sterile. The production of young was the function of the merging of a Power Giver and a Healer.

A Far Seer did not indulge in frivolous thought, but when One Alone looked at his Dear Companion and speculated about the effect of the aurora on her, he could not restrain himself to the spirit of true, scientific inquiry. Was it possible that the aurora could bring maturity to her infantile mind? Would it make her capable of learning? Would her motor coordination center develop so that she would become mobile, able to leave her sleep rack to walk, see him, have the mentality and awareness of an adult?

As he felt sleep search him out, a thought brought him back to tense wakefulness. It was a thought so alien to him that he spent the rest of the sleepless night in self-examination. If his Dear Companion were made whole with eyes to see, if she developed conscious intelligence and awareness she would see him as he was: squat, hairless, eyeless, his pointed dome bald and ugly.

Shocked, he knew that he had just come into a new understanding of the ego of the Old Ones.

"Foolishness," he said, and for the first time in his life he engaged in dreaming. Dear Companion would change, but so would he. She would see him, but he would also see her. They would be Keeper and Far Seer together, as always. She would be a true companion, able to engage in stimulating exchanges of thought.

"You go far afield, Far Seer," he warned himself.

Dear Companion was in one of her wakeful periods. She made happy sounds, then yearning, inviting sounds. His blood stirred, but he did not go to her.

CHAPTER FIFTEEN

And lo, on the morning of the second day of her new life, Cecile of Xanthos created a city. It wasn't a large city. She chose it for its manageable size.

She had not slept. She had no need for sleep. When she felt fatigue, she scanned her body down through the cellular level, refreshed herself, and continued the absorbing exploration of the depths of her mind. There seemed to be no end to the magic that she could do. When she was hungry, she envisioned food and it came to her from the ship's galley ready to eat.

It took a great deal of preparation and mental effort to reassemble the city, but she was to discover that it was more difficult to make an orange. Compared to making an orange from scratch, putting the city back together was simple. She rebuilt the city while the others slept. She stood on a rise of barren rock, dressed in armor, looked down on the rubble heaps, set her mind to work and watched the dead city rise in splendor. The style of architecture was vibrant, soaring. It seemed alien at first, but as she examined the tall, graceful buildings the strangeness of designs became understandable.

The orange was a different matter. To raise the city

she used original materials. It was like putting together a jigsaw puzzle. Making an orange was a much more complicated puzzle with many of the pieces missing. She pictured an orange and nothing happened. She began to draw atoms and molecules from the air, which required a minute study of a real orange from the ship's stores. In the end she had to borrow organic matter from existing items aboard *Paulus,* and then the orange didn't taste exactly right.

The reconstruction of the city served several purposes. First, it was an exercise in getting to know the new Cecile. Second, it would tell her more about the people who had carved the bas-relief in the cave. Last, but not least in importance, it was fun. She was as pleased with her gift as a child celebrating Christmas and her birthday all at once.

Remembering One Alone's fears that she might misapply some unknown power, she experimented with reversing the building process. It was more tiring to disassemble than to assemble. She was relieved to discover that she could destroy only those things that she had constructed.

She was aware that her fellow expedition members were drawing away from her, whether in awe or resentment, but she had no time for such petty concerns. She was in the process of learning, and she was in a hurry because, superperson that she was, she was a parlor magician when compared to the people of the cave. The power of her mind did not put her in the same league with a being who straddled the galaxy and held a sun in his hand.

As she waited for the others to awaken to see her city she tried to destroy a small paperweight. She willed it to shatter into tiny particles, as the surface contents of twenty worlds had been shattered. When nothing happened, she accepted her limitations. It was more rewarding to build, or rebuild.

With the morning, she was rewarded for her labors by amazement, by gasps of astonishment and pleasure. She demonstrated how it was done and the more she worked the easier it became. She tried to explain the process to One Alone.

"I do as we did," she told him. "I visualize an earlier time, see the city, study its patterns and will it to be."

The city had no streets, only open spaces. There were no mechanical means of transportation. Outside entrances to the buildings were set on all levels.

"They soared, like Stella," Clear Thought said.

"The open spaces were parks," John said.

Cecile's ability stopped short of making even so much as a blade of grass.

"Well, she's not God," Martha said to John. "She can't create life."

LaConius was wildly excited. John moved about the city aiming his light recorder with a lump in his throat generated by the beauty of the architecture and the decor. The grace of line and the delicacy of exterior decorations moved him, and then he went into a building to see magnificent artworks and was emotionally overcome. He could almost hate the people who created such loveliness as much as those who destroyed it.

After the initial excitement everyone except Cecile came together in somber silence. The images of the dead were everywhere. Clothing and personal effects gave eloquent testimony to the fact that intelligent, attractive, beauty-loving people had lived in the city.

When they explored a dwelling place they felt like trespassers. It was as if the people who lived in the splendid suite of rooms were temporarily away and might return at any moment to demand an explanation for their intrusion. That thought was moderately intimidating, since it seemed quite likely that the Dead Worlders had been superhuman. Even without their mental powers the men, judging from their clothing, had been almost seven feet tall.

Cecile, alone in more ways than one, sifted time and lifted from it intricate patterns of material things. Luxury was everywhere. Never in known history, not even on Selbelle III, had people lived so well.

One Alone called a conference. He did not insist when Cecile chose to ignore him. The others gathered in a delightful ground level room.

"We're wasting time," LaConius complained. "We're in the middle of an archaeologist's dream—"

"Or a treasure hunter's paradise," Martha said, as she examined a necklace of emeralds.

"—and now is no time to sit around and talk," LaConius continued.

"I am concerned," One Alone said, "that we are rushing headlong into a situation that we will not be able to control."

"Where's the danger?" LaConius asked. "Look at this city, One Alone. It represents an ultimate. There are no slums, no industrial complexes. There's only space and beauty. We're in a little Utopia and there is wealth beyond the comprehension of a Tigian and you are concerned."

"One Alone," Martha said, "I'm a little vague on space law. Don't we have the right of discovery?"

"That's a moot question at the moment," the Far Seer said. "I would guess that the right of discovery would belong to the first man to chart the planet. That goes back several thousand years."

"But this wasn't here in the past when others were here," Martha said, holding up the emeralds.

"The lawyers would have a fine time with that question," Clear Thought said. "The dust to which it was reduced was here. It could be claimed, I'd guess, that the dust was included in the original discovery rights."

The discussion had captured LaConius' interest. "A good claim could be made that salvaging the artifacts would fall under mining rights, or the rights of exploiting natural resources." His eyes hardened. "I will guarantee you this. We'll have our share of all this, if I have to hire every lawyer in the Tigian system."

"With just what's in a few of these buildings," Martha said, "I could finance the reclamation of Terra II."

LaConius was looking around, making estimates of what individual items might fetch at auction on a rich U.P. world.

One Alone admitted to himself that it was not a good time to try to have a logical discussion. He withdrew and the explorations continued.

Stella soared over the city to enjoy an overall view. The others spread out and separated. LaConius encountered Cecile in a large, open space. She had turned off her communicator. She was so self-absorbed that she was startled when LaConius tapped on her helmet.

"Hello, witch," LaConius said.

She did not acknowledge his greeting. Her green eyes stared at him coldly.

"Why don't you use your magic to restore the atmosphere so that we can get out of this armor?" LaConius asked jokingly.

It took a while. It made her very tired. Oxygen had to be freed from rocks and water. Carbon dioxide had to be broken down and poison gases neutralized by separation of molecules. She worked on into the night without the others being aware that slow changes were taking place. The job seemed to be too much for her, but in the middle of the night she discovered that she had to use only a part of her mind, and that once begun the purification process could be made self-sustaining.

It began to rain. By morning water was collecting on the surface. Cecile was waiting for the others when they gathered in the main hut in body armor.

"You don't need the suits," Cecile said.

Clear Thought had not been outside. He went into the air lock and activated it, came back in a couple of minutes. "The atmosphere is just below Xanthos standard," he said. He looked at Cecile, waiting for an explanation.

"It will be Xanthos standard very soon," she said. "We're going back to the caves this morning."

"The hell you say," LaConius yelled.

"Cone, you asked me to restore the atmosphere," Cecile said. "I did. You can breathe the air now. Trust me."

LaConius opened his mouth to protest, decided to be silent. They crowded into a scout and landed near the entrance to the secondary cavern. Inside, Cecile, more confident in her role as restorer, took only a few minutes to bring the domed chamber back to its original condition.

"My God," LaConius said, "it's a brothel."

"Perhaps a temple," John suggested.

Thick carpeting covered the stone floor. Artworks were everywhere. There was one central theme, the celebration of the beauty of the inhabitants of the world, and the secondary theme was erotic. In partitioned alcoves were silken couches, chairs, and raised platforms to serve as beds.

"What a party," LaConius said, as he examined one erotic scene after another.

"Was this what they became?" Stella asked. "Did they have nothing to do except abandon themselves to this?"

"There was a certain lack of modesty," John said, "but there are places on the outworlds where nudity and, ah, open displays of affection are not considered immoral."

"There was no regard at all for privacy," Martha said.

"This may have been the meeting place for a minority cult," Clear Thought said. "We've seen no evidence of such practices in the city."

"Perhaps modesty is peculiar to the human race," John speculated.

"No," Martha said. "We know from the *Book of Miaree* that the loss of ethical values, particularly in the field of sexual behavior, contributed to the downfall of the Artounee race."

LaConius laughed. "Maybe these dudes screwed themselves into oblivion."

"Crude," Martha said, waggling a finger at LaConius.

LaConius grinned. "We send home for a couple of

freighters, cut these carvings away from the walls, load up all the statues and the furnishings and ship them to Xanthos and decorate a fancy restaurant with them. We'd have to have guards at the door to keep the place from being mobbed."

John got into the spirit of the joke. "We'll have a female topless orchestra playing sensuous music on a stand directly under the big picture."

"No good," Martha said. "When a man is exuding male harmones, food is the last thing on his mind."

"Listen to the expert," LaConius said.

"I doubt that X&A would permit removal of artifacts," One Alone said dryly, failing to understand the humor.

Martha giggled, and it became contagious. John said, "Cone, we've got to be unselfish. We can't put great works of art in a greasy spoon restaurant just to make money. What we should do is donate the most graphic of the statuary groupings to the university with one condition—that they be used to decorate the girls' dorms."

"No good," LaConius said, "you'd have a rash of failures among the coed population because the girls would stay up all night studying the wrong subject."

Cecile laughed with them. "I can imagine the face of the Dean of Women when we unveil one of those groupings."

For a while Cecile was one of them again, but she was the worker of magic, the giver of gifts. By the time they arrived back at the city, she was withdrawn.

It was now possible to work without space armor. They lost themselves in the intriguing task of cataloging and recording not individual artifacts, for there were too many of them, but types and classes of objects. One Alone saw that the work was an escape for them, an excuse to forget, for the moment, that there was a superbeing among them. But he did not fail to note that Martha continued to think of the aurora on DW-19, and he knew that time was passing, that the mass of color would bloom again and soon afterward flare up to encompass all of the worlds in the sac.

"No problem getting our degrees now," LaConius said after a full day of exploration during which Stella had lifted each of them into apartments high above the ground level.

John was struck by the triviality of thinking of a degree when the riches of a world lay before them for the taking. It was all too big, too sudden, too frightening when one stopped to think about it. The work was stability. Making notes for his thesis prevented him from thinking about the aurora, and what would happen if he went back to DW-19 and stood in the open during a display.

John's main work was making light recordings. It was Martha who pointed out the scarcity of utilitarian things.

"There are no tools," she said. "There are combs and brushes and other personal care items, and there are eating utensils. There are no shovels, no hammers, no needles, no vehicles, no manufacturing plants."

"Each individual could make anything he wanted," Clear Thought said.

John found a musical instrument in one high apartment to which he had been lifted by Stella. It was complicated. He was from a planet of artists and musicians, and he could bring forth only a discordant, metallic twang. He asked Cecile for help, but she had no feel for music.

"Well, at least we know that not everyone in this society was a painter or a sculptor," John said. "There was at least one musician."

"Which brings up another subject," Martha said. "Why are there no books?"

"We're looking for books as we know them," Clear Thought said. "There may be books here, but not in a printed or an electronically stored form." He held up a small metal ball. "For example, there are dozens of these in most apartments along with a lot of other objects whose purpose we don't know."

"Do you get any vibes from the balls?" LaConius asked Cecile.

"No," she said.

"If they had no written language, it would be understandable," One Alone contributed. "We of Old Earth had neither alphabet nor numbers system."

"Another question," Martha said. "Where are the cemeteries?"

"Lots of possibilities there," John said. "Maybe they were immortal."

"Except in the event of total destruction," Martha said.

"Maybe they burned their dead or reduced them to individual atoms," John went on.

"Cecile, could you make a survey of the surrounding countryside looking for tomb sites?" Clear Thought asked.

Cecile nodded.

"I'd like to locate the administrative center of this

city," Martha said. "If they kept records at all, they'd be there."

"Would a society of supermen need government?" Cecile asked.

John sighed. "Lots of questions. Few answers."

"Cecile, why don't you just rebuild one of those dudes so that we can talk to him."

Cecile didn't answer.

"Come to think of it, make it a woman."

"Not even if I could," Cecile said, with a visible shudder.

"Yes, I suppose that would be a bad idea," LaConius said. "She might want to take over."

No one laughed. Aboard *Paulus* One Alone searched space toward DW-19, the world of the aurora. The lights in the northern sky were strong and growing.

CHAPTER SIXTEEN

The Iboni family could trace its history for no more than a dozen generations. That was not unusual among the best families in the U.P. At one time or another family roots were stretched to breaking by the tyranny of distance. When colonization ships went out to new planets, the ship's data banks contained information more vital to the success of the colony than family genealogies.

When LaConius met someone who claimed to be able to trace his family line back into antiquity, he took that assertion with a healthy portion of doubt. Often such people were only deluding themselves. Actually, to be able to go back twelve generations was unusual, and was possible for the Ibonis because of a certain family vigor. From the time the first Iboni broke his spacer's contract and jumped ship to grab land on a sparsely settled planet in the newly opened Tigian system, Ibonis had been doers.

The founder of the Iboni dynasty on Tigian was Franklin, a ship's metallurgist. He put his knowledge to work for a merchant named Fletcher, married Fletcher's daughter, Elizabeth, and begat John and Evert and several female children. John followed in his father's footsteps and perfected techniques of mining metals on the scorched surface of one of the inner planets of Tigian II. It was John who made the Iboni family one of means. John's son, another Franklin, served in the Tigian parliament, thus establishing a tradition of public service.

Another John—the Ibonis were not too original in selecting names for their male offspring until the father of the current heir married an outworlder who bewitched him into abandoning solid, traditional names to call their son LaConius—expanded the Iboni financial empire to all of the Tigian worlds through a series of brilliant innovations in metallurgy and insured the survival of Iboni wealth as long as the bloodline continued.

Looking back, LaConius had to admit that there'd been a couple of misfires in the glorious line. Carbone Iboni had risked the family wealth in a senseless trade war with powerful Xanthos, taking wild gambles where gambles were unnecessary since the Iboni fortune was large enough and secure enough for anyone except a man of swollen ambitions like Carbone. Actually, LaConius rather admired Carbone for having had the guts to go nose-to-nose with the most powerful commercial cartels in the U.P. Not only did he accept the challenge, he gave the Xanthos interests a run for their money before he avoided total ruin with the aid of an antique projectile hand weapon pointed at his left temple.

Garvel Iboni, Carbone's son, started a rebuilding process that lasted for four generations. Another Franklin, LaConius' grandfather, left an intact financial empire to LaConius' father, still another John, who had proven to be the most ambitious and talented of the line. If John Iboni were to choose to buck the strongest interests on Xanthos he would, in all probability, win.

To LaConius the First—and the last, he was fond of saying, since he would not saddle any of his sons with the name—family was a prime consideration. Loyalty to family was top priority. Being an Iboni meant accepting responsibility. Musing alone in the captain's suite aboard *Paulus,* LaConius considered what the addition of Dead World treasures would do for the Iboni family. He had no doubt he would be the richest man in the known galaxy if, with the help of the best lawyers in the Tigian system, he could figure out a way to possess the captain's share of the treasures that Cecile was busily re-creating.

It was not by chance that the Iboni family was powerful. If luck were involved, it had to do only with the Iboni trait of going far afield for wives, thus keeping the Iboni genes vital enough to continue to produce individuals capable of performing at a high level of achievement. That LaConius was a superior man was beyond question, but he didn't let that spoil his pleasing personality. Ibonis were masters of people skills. He was, he felt, quite liberal with those whom he had invited to join him on the Dead Worlds expedition, and he would not deprive them of their share of the profits. They would simply have to understand that his needs were greater, therefore his share would be larger. After all, he would be head of his family someday, and he would carry the heavy responsibility of running the Iboni financial and industrial empire. Millions of people would depend on him for their jobs and their livelihood. Moreover, he would be expected to carry on the tradition of public service, and running for office could be expensive. Anyone who objected to receiving a smaller share than his would simply have to count his blessing and look to the future when he or she just might need a favor from the most powerful man in the Tigian system.

There were times when LaConius regretted his pre-ordained future. He sometimes felt daunted by the re-sponsibility that would be his. Empire is fragile and subject to the whims of the marketplace, to social change, and to technological advances. Empire, to ex-ist, required continual expansion. Empire was either growing or dying. His would be the task of expanding the Iboni holdings which touched a hundred worlds, and he sometimes felt that was asking too much of one man, even if that man could hire the finest business talent in the U.P. and have the power of billions of credits behind him. After all, he would be the man who had to make the final decisions.

LaConius had no choice but to be outstanding, and he was young. He was, he admitted, no genius. He had a serviceable brain, better than some, and he had a great and terrible fear of becoming another Carbone Iboni. He worried, and he prayed often that he would not bring shame to the family name.

His worry had been groundless. If any single charac-teristic marked an Iboni, it was the ability to see an op-portunity, seize it, and run with it. Never in history had an Iboni had an opportunity with greater potential than that presented to LaConius the First—and, what the heck, maybe not the last. In Cecile alone LaConius had an instrument that could be used to spread the power of Iboni across the galaxy. With Cecile he could kick as much Xanthos ass as he wanted to kick, but that was small stuff. That was pocket change.

His was a grander vision. He was not going to be content just to hire Cecile to work magic for the Iboni Companies. He, himself, the future head of the family, simply had to be in possession of the same mental magic. Old One Alone was being coy about it, but an idiot could have figured out that Cecile's transformation was the result of exposure to the aurora on DW-19. Moreover, LaConius was certain that Cecile had used her magic, her witchcraft, on him to get him away from DW-19 before he had the opportunity to join her in Supermanville. At first he had worried that he'd missed his chance, but he had used the ship's optics to monitor DW-19 and twice he had seen the planet blaze in color, the second time more impressively than the first.

One Alone was a problem. The bureaucrats on Xanthos had insisted that the Far Seer have veto power on the decisions of the expedition's young captain in the name of safety, but it was his ship, his father's money, his expedition. He would not expose the others to danger, lest he be in violation of the X&A permit, but as a free citizen of autonomous Tigian he had every right to expose himself. He required permission from no one.

He programmed the small blink generator of the Number One scout so that it was ready to jump at a moment's notice. Since there were no X&A or planetary patrols on DW-3 to reprimand him for blinking inside the gravity well of a planet, he had only to get into the scout, button up the hatch, push one button, and he would be positioned at ten thousand feet over the north pole of DW-19 in the heart of the aurora.

He chose not to tell anyone of his intent. He joined them in the daily work, but he carried a pocket pager linked to the ship's computer. The computer would notify him of the beginning of another auroral display.

As it happened he was in the scout alone, lifting toward *Paulus* with a selection of artifacts for One Alone's personal examination, when his pager beeped at him and the ship's computer notified him of pre-auroral activity on DW-19. He pushed the button and the scout was flying instantly through the slowly building display of color. He wanted maximum exposure. He opened the scout to the chill air. The cold prickled his skin. Electrical discharges caused his hair to separate strand by strand and stand up straight. The aurora spread up and over him, immersing him totally in color. He endured the cold. He held the scout at the heart of the display. When the aurora faded and dropped away, he was shivering, but aside from being half frozen, he felt no different. He tried a few of Cecile's tricks. Nothing. He couldn't move anything with his mind. After blinking back to DW-3, he couldn't read anyone's mind, but One Alone could still read his.

"I had to try," he said defensively.

"I want permission to examine you," the Far Seer said.

"Go ahead, but you're not going to find anything."

After a long silence One Alone said. "There is a difference."

"Tell me," LaConius said eagerly.

"In wave generation in the forebrain, just as it happened in Cecile and Stella."

"But I can't *do* anything," LaConius wailed.

"It's too early to tell," One Alone said. "Be careful."

Bitterly disappointed, LaConius docked with *Paulus*, went to his suite, threw himself across his bed. Why had Cecile changed? Why had she been singled out?

He stared moodily at a Selbellian metal painting on the wall. It was one of John's works, and he liked it very much. And the damned thing was moving.

He sat up with a jerk. He thought that one of the mind benders, one of the Old Earthers or maybe even Cecile, was doing tricks, but he felt no presence in his mind. Was he just seeing things? He sank back, let his eyes fall once more on the painting, and there was the movement. By God, he was seeing something and the images were affecting a level of his mind that was unfamiliar to him. He moved closer to the painting, stared at it, gave a whoop. The movement he was seeing was a familiar pattern, although he'd never seen it before except in theory. What he was seeing was the interaction of molecules as they expanded with the increase in temperature caused by his body heat and by the light he'd turned on when entering the suite.

His mind soared. He stared at the metallic painting and saw with ease the dance of the molecules. He had a gift, and it wasn't a bad one at all. In fact, it made sense that his own extrasensory perception would have to do with his interest in metals. Ah, the work he could do with metals when he could know them down to the molecular level. That ability alone would make him the greatest metallurgist in history.

He was not content with that one gift for long, however. He found that by expanding his mind he could sense the frantic orbiting of subatomic particles. It took a few minutes before, with his heart pounding, he made his first attempt at manipulating individual molecules and atoms. He didn't want to do something silly, like ripping one of the little bastards apart to release some rather nasty energy. He knew his atomics. He'd work with just one atom. Gently try to examine it. Later, he would try to dismantle an atom into its constituent parts.

He chose a durasteel molecule in the wall and sent mind force at it. The thought cut a neat, round hole in the bulkhead beside John's metallic painting. The hole extended through the insulation cavities, through radiation shields, thorough the twin outer hull. Explosive decompression began instantaneously.

He was dead. He knew that. The hole was too big to be handled by the automatic sealant between the hulls. Alarms were clanging throughout the ship. He heard the clang of metal doors as the ship's systems isolated his suite. He felt the pull of the vacuum of space. Small objects flew toward the hole as air whistled out into emptiness. He was so calm that he was astounded. Time stood still. Hell, this was kid stuff. He pictured processes in the metal of the hull and the metal flowed, filled in the cavity. Only the wood paneling on the bulkhead showed damage. Emergency pumps hummed as air was restored to Xanthos standard pressure in his suite.

He threw back his head and laughed. He was a walking weapon, a living disassembler. But, by God, he could reassemble, too.

He felt the presence of One Alone. "False alarm," he said. "A glitch in the leak detection system."

"Permission to examine," One Alone said.

"Sure." He didn't mind, because One Alone might be of help in understanding the things he could do. He didn't want any more accidents. He demonstrated to One Alone that he could disintegrate and reassemble anything made of metal. He could tune his power to remove microscopic layers. He could hone an edge to the thickness of one molecule. He was, by himself, a new field of metallurgy; and as he and One Alone talked, he discovered that he was the ultimate metal detector, as well. He sent his mind searching down to the planet and below the surface. He could have drawn maps of the subsurface deposits of ore. He could grade the ore in situ. He could locate minute scraps of metal in the rubble heaps.

"My God," he said, "I'm the galaxy's finest mining instrument. I could do a flyby of a planet and map the ore fields."

He was having so much fun that it was a long time before he began to wonder why his abilities were limited to detecting and manipulating metals. He could do no magic with a nonmetallic material. In a fit of pique he ordered a glass to disintegrate. Nothing happened.

"Careful," One Alone warned.

Next day he watched Cecile reassemble a building. He tried to emulate her without success, but he sensed a large deposit of iron ore under the ground. He graded it idly. It was a fine deposit, very rich. On a U.P. planet it would have been well worth exploiting. He toyed with the ore, separating metal, moving molecules. Suddenly there was a peculiar little tug in his forebrain and shapeless blobs of pure iron began to pile up at his feet. He was the ultimate mining machine. He could disassemble iron below the surface and lift it, atom by atom, to be reassembled. He was so stunned that he failed to notice Martha's approach.

Martha watched for a few moments. "Cone, you too?" she asked.

He had not meant for them to know, not just yet.

"But you were not exposed," Martha said.

"No."

"How, then?" she asked.

He said, "I don't know."

"I don't think we should begin to deceive each other," One Alone said.

"I flew over to DW-19 in a scout," LaConius said.

"I think we need to have a group discussion," Martha said. Her face was pale with anger.

Clear Thought, always willing to grant the benefit of the doubt, was not interested in laying blame on LaConius. He wanted to know more about the aurora. "It seems that it changes one according to one's personal interests," he said. "Cecile was interested in architecture. She was given the ability to reconstruct buildings and other artifacts. Stella, although the effects were less because of her protective scales, had her field scanning ability sharpened. LaConius, interested in metals, commands metals."

"I will repeat my warning," One Alone said. "We are dealing with the unknown. I know that each of you is eager to undergo the change, but I think it best to avoid exposure until we know more."

"How will we learn unless we experiment?" Martha asked.

LaConius was wondering what would happen if he were exposed again.

"I have delayed discussion of one aspect of the situation," One Alone said. "Cecile and I, working together, were able to predict that the auroral activity will not be confined to DW-19 alone. The intensity is increasing with each display and it will spread throughout the system in a very short time. I will listen to your opinions, but I warn you that it is my duty to exercise the authority which has been delegated to me by the charter. I am undecided as to the proper course of action, but I will make my decision in a short time whether we all stay to receive maximum exposure or whether we lift away from the sac before the final blossoming."

"I say we stay," Martha said defiantly.

"It will cover the entire system?" John asked. "Including this planet?"

"Yes," One Alone said.

"I'd like to stay, One Alone," John said. He moved to Martha's side, took her hand. "You Old Earthers have your inherited abilities. Cecile and Cone are supermen. Everyone's super except me and Martha."

"I'm staying," Martha said.

CHAPTER SEVENTEEN

Martha was bored with wealth and splendor. She was totally fed up with cataloging item after endless beautiful and luxurious item.

Cecile had gone off alone, as usual, presumably to continue her ceaseless reconstructions. Martha couldn't have cared less. She told John, "When you've seen one fantastically rich, unbelievably beautiful, utterly fantastic alien city, you've seen them all."

There was too much of everything. There were too many diamonds and emeralds and rubies. There was too much gold and too much platinum and silver. It was like visiting a huge, multi-planet museum where the exhibits extended for miles and the eye tired. Her mind was dulled by an excess of beauty; and the godlike perfection of the images of the dead inhabitants made her feel as if she had been slighted by nature by having been formed as merely an attractive girl with a reasonably good mind.

Martha had spent her formative years on a planet that had been plundered and poisoned by man in his eagerness to get back into space. If there was one usable ounce of any metal left in ore form on Terra II, it would take a magician like LaConius to find it. Any di-

amond left on Terra II would be so deeply hidden in
the bowels of the earth that it could only be extracted
by a planet buster. In Cecile's city she was surrounded
by riches. She was rich. She could reach out her hand
and pick up objects that would fetch billions of credits
on any U.P. world. All that, and no place to spend it.
Moreover, considering what the Dead Worlds had done
for Cecile and LaConius, just being rich was not
enough. Cecile could build herself a world, if she
chose to do so. LaConius could become the richest
man in the universe.

With Cecile's powers she could rebuild Terra II. With
LaConius' gift she could find enough wealth to hire the
rebuilding done. Eventually the riches of DW-3 would
help her return her own world to its original beauty, but
it would be so slow. She loved Terra II too much to be
content with conventional methods. She wanted to be
able to purify the atmosphere almost instantly, as Cecile
had done on DW-3. She wanted to see Terra II as it had
been when the first settlers landed. She wanted to be
able to walk through huge, virgin forests of hardwoods, to
swim in clear streams, breath air so pure that it tingled in
the lungs.

If she could convince Cecile to go home with her,
Cecile could work swift miracles. She could remove
the last of the pollutants from the air and the water, reconstruct selected historic sites such as the Museum of
Life, where once some of the animal and plant life-
forms of Old Earth had been bred from seed and em-
bryos that had survived the destruction of the
colonization ship. Pictures of the building were available. It would be but the work of a moment for Cecile
to restore it to its former magnificence. It was said that

the odd columns and decorated pediments of the building were copied from memory of an Old Earth architectural style.

Martha's home was in the foothills of an eroded mountain range. On a slope below the old observatory that had been restored by her father was a country estate with a manor house in an advanced state of decay. She had always dreamed of rebuilding the house. To live there with clean air and clear water had been her fondest wish.

But, given Cecile's powers, she wouldn't be selfish. She would continue to work to restore the planet and open it to selected settlement, or, at worst, allow tour groups to visit the planet that was mankind's second home, the first planet to be settled.

One Alone was concerned about side effects caused by exposure to the aurora. Martha was rapidly coming to the point where she was willing to take the risk. She saw no ill effects in LaConius or Cecile. She wanted her chance. She felt that she deserved it as much as any of the others.

"It isn't fair," she complained to John.

"I don't know," John said. "I have a lot of confidence in One Alone's judgment. For the moment I'm going to take his advice."

"And what if the aurora stops and we miss the opportunity?" she asked.

She knew John well. Their relationship went back three full years. Early on, when they realized that their mutual attraction had a potential for permanence, they agreed to complete work on their terminal degrees before forming a family unit. There were problems that would have to be faced, not the least of which was where they would live. John wanted to live and work on his home planet, among other artists, but his number one priority was to make his mark in the artistic world.

"John, you have the chance to become the galaxy's greatest creative artist," she said. "Are you willing to pass up that chance because One Alone is concerned about side effects?"

"You know which button to push, don't you?" he asked her.

"We're the only ones left who have no special ability. The Old Earthers have theirs. Cecile has—well whatever it is. LaConius can be the richest man in the universe. What will we be?"

"Has it occurred to you how calmly we have accepted some rather odd events?" He was serious. "We didn't turn a hair when Cecile began working magic. We shrugged when LaConius separated metal from matrix rock and brought it to the surface. Now and then I wonder if I shouldn't be just a little bit afraid of Cecile, but then I look around and see the city and I accept it. Why?"

She shrugged. "We're all sane. We are mature enough to accept what we see with our own eyes."

"No one, not even One Alone, has wondered what is happening to those of us who haven't been exposed to the aurora. We're changed. There are twenty worlds here in the sac and they're all very, very dead. I think that if we were thinking normally we'd all be running like hell, screaming for help. If we're not the victims of mass hallucinations, we have physical proof that the people of this world, at least, were beautiful and talented. They seem to have had everything, but they're dead. I think we should ask a lot of questions before we let Cecile continue, or before the rest of us take a bath in the aurora."

"Perhaps the answers lie in the aurora," Martha said.

"Cecile used to be a happy person. She was the fun girl among us. She enjoyed life. Have you seen her smile lately?"

"That's Cecile," Martha said defiantly. "That's like someone saying money can't buy happiness. I think I could be a very happy rich lady, and I think I could handle some of the extrasensory abilities that the aurora imparts. I know that I do not want to leave here without having my chance to see what the aurora will do for me."

"I won't enter into the kind of deception that LaConius used," John said. "I'm not going to sneak off to DW-19. I think we should get together with the others and discuss the situation."

"I will vote that we allow each individual to make his own choice," she said.

"Fair enough," he said.

"What do you think Cecile and LaConius will say?" she asked.

"I don't know."

"They have theirs," she said. "And Stella was exposed and nothing happened. I think Clear Thought is curious enough to want to try it. One Alone might try to stop us."

"We'll have to wait and see," he said.

Martha called for a conference with all expedition members present. John seconded it, making it mandatory under the charter. One Alone, physically present, opened the meeting.

"I want you to have all available information," he

said, "before we discuss future plans. Although I can't explain the phenomenon of the aurora, I can tell you that it is made up of an electromagnetic field formed not only by DW-19, but by all of the stars and other bodies in the sac system. The field is quite complicated at any given time, but under cyclical conditions that occur every 75,000 New Years, it takes on a character that results in the auroral display."

Martha, eager to get on with it, leaned forward.

"We have plenty of time, daughter," One Alone said. "The field is growing stronger, not weaker. We are not yet at the point in time when the display flares out through space to touch all of the sac system planets."

Martha relaxed.

"Since it is estimated that the destruction of the twenty worlds in this system coincided with the last occurrence of the particular configuration that produces the aurora, there is at least circumstantial evidence that both the swift rise of the cities on the sac planets and their destruction may be linked to the aurora and its effects."

"I can't agree with that," Martha said. "Cecile can't destroy. She can only remake something that has been devastated."

"And LaConius?" One Alone asked.

"He can shoot a hole through metal," Martha said with a shrug.

"And what will he be able to do if we remain here and are exposed to the full intensity of the aurora?" One Alone asked grimly. "This is what we must consider."

"How long do we have?" John asked.

"The displays of color will flare out from DW-19 to

planets 9, 7, and 18 within the next few days," One Alone said. "The climactic engulfment of the entire system will occur in three standard months less a day and a few hours."

"When will the aurora reach this planet?" Martha asked.

"A few days."

"You're being coy, One Alone," Martha said. "Let me get this straight. The aurora will last for another three months and then it won't happen again for 75,000 New Years?"

"That is correct," One Alone said.

Martha looked at John. "Since it's highly unlikely that we'll be around 75,000 years from now, it's now or never for us, isn't it?"

"That, too, is correct," One Alone said. "I must confess that I have formed my opinions in advance, but I think we should consider all options. For example, if we move swiftly, we can take *Paulus* to the nearest blink beacon and blinkstat a message to Xanthos. Perhaps there would be an X&A ship close enough to put scientists in position to study the aurora before it reaches its climax."

"You're not willing to risk our exposure, but you want to create dozens of supermen who just happen to be in the crew of an errant X&A exploration ship?" Martha asked.

"Not a chance," LaConius said, his voice soft.

"That is only one option," One Alone said. "I would be against taking such a step. I am, as you say, reluctant to risk exposing you, who are my friends. I would not accept the responsibility of exposing dozens."

"What are your reservations about our exposing ourselves?" Clear Thought asked.

"I am concerned mostly with your safety."

"Not with adding to the population of supermen?" Clear Thought asked.

"I'm sure that you don't have to be reminded that I am a Far Seer, and that my entire being is devoted to the welfare of humanity. However, I, too, am human in my own way. You are my friends. I know each of you well, since you modified the rules of privacy for this expedition, allowing me to collect data unobserved. I do not detect in any of you the sickness of power hunger. None of you is perfect, mind you—"

"Ahhhhh," John moaned in mock disappointment.

"—but there is in each of you a measure of consideration for your fellow men, an innate goodness. That is why I have allowed myself to list as one option the exposure of this entire group."

"Yes," Martha said with fervor.

"I follow you," LaConius said. "We're compatible. We're fairly decent people. We make a good test group. On the other hand, in spite of X&A personality testing if we called in an X&A ship there could be a borderline psychopath aboard and God only knows what would happen if some nut case who had slipped through the bureaucratic cracks got irradiated into being—"

"Like you, Cone," John said.

"That is one of my considerations," One Alone said. "There is a possibility that the destruction of twenty worlds was the work of one maladjusted individual. I am torn by the decision. As Martha so vividly points out, this opportunity will not come again for 75,000 years. What if, by not calling for an X&A ship and, thus, by not exposing a wider collection of personalities to the aurora we lose the opportunity to heal mankind of all ailments, or to extend the life span significantly? What if nature intended the extreme speed up of evolution that comes from exposure to the aurora and we delay her plans for another 75,000 years?"

"What if, by exposing yourself," Cecile asked quietly, "you can see the face of your Dear Companion with human eyes?"

One Alone's head jerked toward Cecile, but he remained silent.

"We're a small cross section of humanity," Martha said. "We have an almost equal number of Old Ones and New Ones. We know each other well enough so that we can trust each other. By exposing all seven of us we'll probably have a variety of talents, if what happened to LaConius and Cecile is the rule. Seven of us, with superpowers, can do a lot for mankind."

"Eight," One Alone said.

"Yes, I'm sorry," Martha said. "I tend to consider Dear Companion a part of you, One Alone. No one in this group is going to go psycho. None of us will do anyone any harm."

"At least not intentionally," Stella said.

"What do you mean?" Martha asked.

"The odd accident," Stella said. "We were all dead once, although some of you may not have realized it. It happened when Cecile and One Alone were trying to measure the strength of Cecile's mind. You know that LaConius cut a hole in the ship's hull when he was trying out his new power."

LaConius grinned. "But I fixed it quickly."

"We're all aware of the danger now," Martha said. "We can proceed with great care."

"I agree," Clear Thought said, "that none of us would do harm intentionally."

Martha rose and paced nervously. "I'm beginning to feel like a poor space gypsy child standing outside a bakery shop watching people go in and come out with bagsful of goodies. I want a cookie, too."

"The possibilities are interesting," LaConius said. "We all expose ourselves. We work out what powers we have and figure out how best to use them. We pool our talents. For example, we could find a borderline planet and build it up. Cecile gives it air. I mine metals to finance all of it. You others do your thing, whatever it turns out to be."

"To make profit for the Iboni financial holdings?" Martha asked.

LaConius grinned. "Profit is the prime motive." He became serious. "Look, what's the rarest thing in the galaxy? A good, sweet water world in a sun's life zone. There are sorry planets in multiples of good ones. Many of those uninhabitable ones could be converted to human use by just me and Cecile. If exposure gives you others different talents, there's no limit to what we can do."

"Those are worthy thoughts," Clear Thought said.

"Let's go for it," Martha said eagerly. "Let's go all out, take the full dose. I vote that we fly over to DW-19 and get started now. Today."

"Let me suggest one alternate course," One Alone said. "Let us use the time before the aurora reaches this planet to think and plan. We have a large body of information now, thanks to Cecile, but we have no direct insight into the people who lived on this world. We've talked about the possibility of their having some way to store information. Let us work as long and as hard as we can to discover that secret. I would feel much more comfortable about exposing this group to the aurora if we knew more about what happened here 75,000 years ago."

"I'll go along with that," John said quickly. Clear Thought and Stella agreed.

"I don't think anyone else should sneak off and expose himself," Martha said.

"And I don't think anyone, including you, One Alone, should think any more about sending a blinkstat," LaConius said.

"No," One Alone said. "At least not for the moment."

CHAPTER EIGHTEEN

The days following the conference in the lounge of the *Paulus* were busy, the work repetitive. The people of DW-3 had liked the glow of precious metals, the gleam of jewels, the sheen of fine fabrics. They had left evidence of their artistic worth in glass, crystal, metal, paint, ceramics, textiles, wood, and stone; and almost every artifact had been made to please one or more of the senses. The furnishings of the luxurious living areas were among the few items that seemed to have a practical, physical purpose. There were no appliances for cooking. There were no tools.

"Think and it shall be," Clear Thought said, in an effort to explain, for one thing, the lack of manufacturing facilities. "Want and you shall have. Desire and be fulfilled."

One Alone had long since come to the same conclusion. He was puzzled by a society that was productive only in the fields of gratification. He was not yet ready to judge the morality of the departed alien race, but he was disturbed by the preponderance of eroticism in the art objects that were present in each dwelling in great number.

In *The Book of Rack The Healer* there was a cryptic

reference which had led to many debates among Healers and Far Seers on Old Earth. One Alone felt that the excerpt had never been fully understood simply because members of the Old Earth society had no frame of reference against which to measure the concept. The quotation of which One Alone was reminded was attributed to Rose the Healer and it pertained to the Old Ones in the last days before the Destruction. Rose the Healer said that the morality of humanity consisted of one adage: *What thou will shall be the whole of the law.*

After he came into contact with the Old Ones following the reunification of the race, One Alone felt that he understood Rose's intended explanation of the morality of the Old Ones; but it was only on DW-3 that he came to comprehend the concept of a life of total abandon. If one were to believe the evidence in the form of the erotic art, the people of DW-3 had no regard for privacy. The intimate relationship between male and female that Old Earthers called blending had no sanctity on DW-3.

When the Old Earthers came into contact with the unmutated descendants of their own ancestors, the Old Ones, the reunification was not without trauma to both divisions of the race. For the Old Earthers it was a shock to find that the females of the Old Ones could bear children repeatedly; but it was more of a cultural jolt to discover that Old Ones often prevented by artificial means the sacred union of sperm and ova and that they shared with Far Seers and their Keepers the dubious dispensation of being free to copulate for pleasure alone.

One Alone reviewed all of the early records stored in

the mind of his Dear Companion. He reread the private thoughts of Far Seers who had been involved in the rejoining of the two elements of the race. He mused over the sexual attitudes of the Old Ones, and was reminded of his horror when he first knew that the Old Ones killed life, in the form of animals, for food. On Old Earth the prime food source had been a sea plant. In the great, outside universe of the United Planets Confederation, Old Earthers had found a cornucopia of vegetable matter suitable for their metabolism. To any Old Earther life was sacred and the death of any animal was a sadness. It had taken him a long time to accept the Old Ones' practice of eating flesh. Even if his body could have accepted meat as food, he would not have eaten of a slaughtered animal, but he could not deny that practice to the Old Ones, since it was their nature.

Could he, in time, accept the apparent sexual abandon of the people of DW-3 as he had accepted the practices of the Old Ones? He longed for a council of Far Seers so that with a merger of minds he could be aided in searching the past for guidance. In the absence of others of his peers, however, he called on Clear Thought and Stella.

Healers had always been the most liberal members of the Old Earth race. He agreed with One Alone that the artistic works of the dead ones indicated a certain quality of free thinking regarding sexual matters. "I don't think, however, that we should judge their code of ethics entirely by evidence that they partook of physical pleasures."

Neither Clear Thought nor Stella mentioned that they had discussed between themselves the desirability of being allowed more than one mating in a lifetime. Such talk represented dreams and speculation about what might happen to them if and when they were exposed to the full force of the aurora.

"I think that the indolence of these people might be more indicative of their racial character than their sexual habits," Clear Thought said.

Healers were doers. Idleness or activity for the sake of amusement only was questionable, to say the least, to Clear Thought.

"But isn't it understandable?" Stella asked. "They had no need to work. If there is unlimited luxury, if nothing is needed, is it immoral not to work? We don't know what they did, or what they thought, so can we criticize them? Surely not for their desire for nice things. Everyone would sleep on silk if it were readily available."

"But never to strive for achievement?" Clear Thought asked.

"Perhaps they fulfilled that need through their art," Stella said.

"Never to aspire to—" Clear Thought did not finish the thought. He shrugged his scaled shoulders. "Men, and I mean the entire race, have always been workers by nature."

"By nature of their needs," Stella said. "We've been forced to work to get food. The Old Ones planted and reaped, not because it pleased them but because they had to eat."

"And brew beer," Clear Thought said.

"All right," she said. "But it was all based on need. The system of barter grew because one man couldn't produce everything he needed, or wanted, and from that came monetary systems. It became possible for one man to amass more than he needed, more than he could ever use, and the concept of riches was born. What I'm getting at is this. A very wealthy man doesn't work. He does exactly what the Dead Worlders did. He enjoys. He buys paintings, jewels, art objects. He buys leisure and amusement. That's exactly what these people did. Apparently everyone could afford anything he wanted because he merely had to think about it and it was."

Clear Thought nodded.

"Everywhere on this world are things of great beauty," Stella said. "It seems to me that these people achieved what man has always strived to accomplish. What are the most treasured works of mankind? Paintings, sculpture, great buildings, music, writings. We admire man's artistic accomplishment over everything else. So, if every man had the ability to have what he wants, where would he then direct his efforts? I'd say toward the making of things of beauty. In this I don't believe the people who lived here were any different from mankind."

"They are dead," One Alone said.

"Yes," Stella admitted.

"I believe, Stella, that you want to stay here until the colors blossom," One Alone said.

"I do, Far Seer," she said.

"And I," Clear Thought added.

One Alone contemplated in solitude in his cabin. The aurora was reaching out from DW-19, waves of color in empty space. Two other planets had been engulfed. He knew that he had only a short time.

He considered the wonder of life. On Old Earth before the destruction there'd been life in every available niche of the ecosystem. The *Miaree* manuscripts indicated that on the Artounee and Delanian worlds there had also been a rich variety of life-forms. But on DW-3 the available evidence, the works of art, showed nothing of animal life. It seemed unlikely to him that the godlike humanoids had developed in total isolation. The thought that animal life had existed but had been beneath the notice of the beautiful people of the world was almost as disturbing as thinking that there'd been only one form of life; and he was bothered by his inability to explain the swiftness of the rise of the humanoids.

Life was a product of nature. Life evolved. The most primitive of life-forms found on the various planets of the U.P. followed the rules of evolution. On DW-3 the plan of nature had been thrown askew by the effects of the aurora, leaving questions, the most pressing of which was what had gone before the beautiful people? Intelligent life could not possibly develop in the period, a mere 75,000 N.Y., between auroral displays, but it seemed that an advanced civilization had arisen and destroyed itself in one cycle. Had a previous cycle seen the birth of primitive forms of life? That there had been vegetative life in the distant past was evidenced by the presence of fossil fuels.

It was impossible to theorize a pattern. Plant life had existed, and had been compressed in the usual geological processes to form coal. Coal and petroleum products were used, however, for only a few thousand years. The millions of years that had been required for man to evolve on Old Earth had been reduced to one 75,000 year cycle, or, possibly, a fraction of one cycle. Then there was perfection and destruction. Did perfection demand obliteration? Was there nothing to follow the ultimate?

One possibility intrigued One Alone. Had the effects of the aurora advanced primitive life so swiftly that the physical characteristics of the race outdistanced their mental advancement? Were those perfect beings imperfect in wisdom, morality, responsibility?

Judging from their images, the Dead Worlders were much like man. They walked erect, had binocular vision, and four fingers plus an opposed thumb. Man, however, was an ancient race. Man's achievements had not come swiftly or easily. Man did not have the gift of getting something for nothing. He had to exercise wisdom to achieve.

One Alone was devout in the belief that the main function of Nature was to support life. He believed that the universe had been created for one purpose, to lead inevitably toward life. The stars, using the building blocks of the creator to make life-giving warmth and energy, had been made to serve life. A star without a family of planets, without the potential for life, was a sad and sterile thing. So, if such was the purpose of the universe, how could he fail to believe that he and his friends of the *Paulus* expedition had been led to the Dead Worlds at such a crucial time for a reason?

He observed the others as they worked on the surface of the planet. He heard laughter. He was witness to youthful enthusiasm where total silence and devastation had reigned for 75,000 N.Y. There was life, and it was his reverence for life that helped him form his final decision. There was laughter and life on a world that had been dead for millennia. There was good air and healing rain. The planet would know more life, and on that world life would be perpetuated. The risk was worth the stake. He was willing to put his own life in the balance along with that of his Dear Companion and the other six. The risk would be minimized by his own ability.

His confidence was not egotistic. He was a Far Seer, and he had certain powers. Under his guidance the group would be safe, and, if changes were made in them, he would be there to see that they did only what was good for the race as a whole.

Once the decision was made there was still time to explore other matters. He singled out John. "Even in a society of telepaths, wouldn't there have been music?" he asked.

"I have been thinking along the same lines," John said.

"And with all of their abilities wouldn't they have had some way of recording that music?"

"I've been looking," John said.

"There is this, too," One Alone said. "We know that they had a concept of written communications because they left us a message carved into the rock of DW-I. We must search for a clue to their language. We must seek out their methods of preserving data, and we have little time."

To Cecile, in privacy, One Alone reached out to find sadness. "Something haunts me," she admitted when he expressed his concern. "It is an awareness just beyond my reach. There are times when I am content, mostly when I'm working to put things back together, but—"

"The other times? When you are not happy?"

"I don't know," she said. "Perhaps it's only a reaction to what's happened."

"May I enter, daughter?"

"Yes," she said, opening her mind.

He felt nameless dread.

"Daughter, do you sense danger?"

"I don't know."

"Would you please open your mind to Dear Companion so that I can study your feelings in detail?"

Cecile always enjoyed contact with the Keeper. While recording her own thoughts she had access to awesomely detailed banks of information. She had at her command the wisdom of the Far Seers, the thoughts of Rose the Healer who had left fragments of poetry, meaningless measurements, a nostalgia for things past. She knew the desperation felt by Rack the Healer as he lay dying.

It was sad, tender, restful to glean the lore of the Far Seers, to know a few remaining lines from the books of the Old Ones; and it was reassuring to feel the love that One Alone had for his Dear Companion. She, in her loneliness, wished for a man to love her as the Far Seer loved his keeper. She would have given up everything for that, and she would have been content.

CHAPTER NINETEEN

The first auroral storm came to DW-3 days before One Alone expected it. It blossomed up from the southern polar regions. The ship's instruments were activated seconds after One Alone was awakened from sleep by the tingling of the magnetic field. He sat up in his rack with his heart pounding.

Only One Alone and Dear Companion were living aboard *Paulus*. The others had taken up palatial quarters in Cecile's city.

Unlike the slow and gradual accretion of the aurora on DW-19 in the beginning, the flowering of color was swift and total on DW-3. Exposure was already underway when One Alone woke Clear Thought, Stella, and Cecile.

"I record in the mind of Dear Companion and in the ship's log that I am calling a council of four," One Alone said. "There is still time to override the decision to risk exposure to the full strength of the aurora. Should the three of you think that my affirmative decision is unwise, I will respect your opinion and we four will prevail over the others."

"I feel no indication that life is at risk," Clear Thought said.

"There is no immediate danger," One Alone agreed.

"I want answers, Far Seer," Clear Thought said.

"And I," Stella said.

"And you, daughter?" One Alone asked Cecile.

"It would be selfish to deny all of you a chance to be changed. That is not, however, my main consideration. I feel that together we can benefit everyone, the race, the human population of the galaxy."

"Then we are agreed," One Alone said. "Wake the others. There is no hurry, for this display will last for a long time."

Grandeur filled the nighttime sky. Soaring, flickering color dimmed the foreboding, heavy, pearl glow of the core that hung over them. They gathered outside the city on a hill where the view of the sky was unimpeded. Stella enclosed Clear Thought in her field of power and soared with him to enter the writhing tendrils of light. Martha held John's hand tightly. She was more nervous than she was willing to admit.

The display was stronger and longer lasting than any they had seen on DW-19. It touched the earth around them, glowed reflections in their eyes.

When it was over, One Alone examined them all. He could find no changes in their brain waves. The character of the aurora had been the same as those that had occurred on DW-19, but the subtle alterations in cerebral activity that marked Cecile and LaConius were absent in the others. There was disappointment, but there would be other nights and there was still plenty of time to blink back to DW-19 where the aurora had changed Cecile and LaConius.

There was little interest in working the next day. There was a sameness to the dwelling places in the

city. In addition to the riches and the beautifully designed decorative objects, each apartment had one or
more small rooms that, judging from the decor, was reserved for sexual activity.

Martha called them all together for lunch in a luxurious room with a long table. LaConius poked around
in the lunch basket and said, "Same old stuff."

"I didn't have time to prepare duckling a la orange,"
Martha said.

"I was planning to use magic and materialize food
the way the tall fellows did," John said, referring to the
former inhabitants of the planet. He was just as disappointed as Martha because of the lack of results after
exposure to the aurora.

"Or just say zap and teleport something decent down
from the ship," LaConius said.

"Nothing to it," Martha said. She stood, held out her
hands. "You see, ladies and gentlemen, that there is
nothing up my sleeve. There will be absolutely no trickery as the lady brings you your choice of gourmet
meals. Place your orders now."

"Roast duckling," LaConius said.

"Your wish is my command," Martha said, playing the
ham to hide her own bitter disillusionment. "Abraca-
dabra, I give you roast duck."

A self-heating container of Belotian roast duck materialized on the table. Martha's face went white. She felt
faint. She sat down suddenly.

LaConius broke the silence. "Did you do that,
Cecile?" he asked.

Cecile shook her head. Martha's face beamed. She
leaped to her feet and danced around the table. "No,"
she shouted, "Cecile did not do that. I did it."

"It came from the *Paulus*," John said.

"I just pictured it on a shelf in cold storage aboard ship and said in my mind, I want that," Martha said.

"I'm hungry," LaConius said.

"How can you be hungry when I've just done a miracle?" Martha demanded.

"It's warm," Cecile said to LaConius. "Let's eat."

"How can you be so blasé?" Martha wailed.

Cecile and LaConius began to eat. One Alone asked Martha's permission to examine her. He found the tell tale differences in her brain waves. She could teleport anything within sight, regardless of weight. She brought down a book from her cabin aboard *Paulus*. She walked to a window, saw a huge boulder on a ridge overlooking the city, lifted it. It broke into parts from the stress of its own weight before she let it fall.

John was not eating. "Can you move a living being?" he asked.

"Shall I try with you?" she asked.

"No," One Alone said swiftly from his cabin aboard ship.

"Then I'll fly," Martha said happily. She soared up, bumped against the ceiling. She flew out an open window and was gone for long minutes. When she came back she cried, "Oh, Stella, it's so wonderful. It's glorious."

There was one more area to be explored. She swallowed, quelled momentary fear, pictured the lounge aboard *Paulus* and was there. Back on the surface she moved John to the ship and brought him back.

One Alone was observing and measuring. Why had only Martha been affected? Why not John, Clear Thought, and Stella?

There was no more work that day. There was a lot of talk, a lot of dreaming. LaConius speculated about the commercial value of Martha's talent. For one thing, he could mine ore from an entire planet and Martha could ship it to a U.P. market at no cost. John, sober, thoughtful, said, "Cone, I'm getting a little tired of hearing you talk about money. You seem to think that Cecile and Martha are doing parlor tricks for your benefit. Don't you realize that we're watching the creation of superhumans? Doesn't it impress you just a little to think that if Martha wanted to, she could zap you into the nearest sun? With what she can do, she could rule the galaxy."

LaConius squinted his eyes in thought.

"I would never do anything to hurt anyone," Martha said. "And I don't care to be the ruler of the galaxy."

"We're not thinking big enough," LaConius said. "The whole universe is open to us."

Martha turned away. She was thinking that she could rule the galaxy unless someone like Cecile or LaConius tried to stop her. She wasn't serious, of course. It was just an exercise in creative thinking. She could catch them both off guard and lift them into the heart of a star, or into the vacuum of space. In doing so, she would risk—what? LaConius could control the molecular and atomic movements of metal. Cecile could reassemble things that had been destroyed.

She *could* rule, but that was just idle speculation.

John, troubled, sought privacy. He found a room with a huge bed and relaxed with his head propped up on a pile of pillows. On a bedside table was a carved stone container holding several odd, multicolored balls whose purpose was unknown. They were light in the hand as if they were hollow and they were the most common of all objects to be found in the dwellings. He reached out, picked up a sphere from the top of the heap, and rolled it in his hand to admire the colors. The ball was smooth and pleasant to hold. Perhaps, he thought, it had significance since it was in the shape of suns, worlds, moons. Perhaps the tall ones had just been a sensuous bunch that took some kind of pleasure in holding the round smooth ball in hand. He rubbed the sphere idly against his forehead. He thought, Well, it's nothing. Just another decorative object, something to feel, something to give pleasure to the eye.

He dropped the ball onto the bed beside him. "Well, it's nothing," a voice said. "Just another decorative object, something to feel, something to give pleasure to the eye."

He knew the voice, for it was his own. He hesitated only a moment. One Alone, he thought. Come to me.

I am here.

Did you hear?

No. I was elsewhere. Relax. Let me see why you're so agitated.

John felt the feathery touch of the Far Seer in his mind. He shared the incident with One Alone and waited.

"I think we've found their method of storing data," John said. He seized the sphere and willed it to repeat his words, but there was only silence.

"Go through it just as you did before," One Alone said.

He placed the sphere against his forehead.

Once mastered, the process was simple. His thoughts were recorded directly into the sphere. After a

few minutes he did not have to place it against his forehead. Upon a calm, mental command the sphere
played back his thoughts vocally.

One Alone knew an excitement that was quite un-
characteristic in a Far Seer. "If you can record your
thoughts, others have done the same in the past," he
said.

"But surely we'll find nothing but empty spheres,"
John said. "Could Cecile reproduce the recorded
thoughts of people who have been dead so long?"

"Please try," One Alone said.

John tried sphere after sphere, willing it to speak in
the voice of the dead.

"They're all blank, empty," he said.

"You sense something," One Alone said. "I can read
in your mind that you feel something."

"I can't—" He paused, laughed. "Is this my great and
magical gift? Is this my power, to be delivered from
writing poems in longhand? If so, I've got a lifetime
supply of dictation machines."

One Alone, eager to monitor the activities of Martha,
withdrew.

John had not chosen to be trained in music. He was
an avid listener, however. One song, a favorite of his,
had never been performed as he felt it should be. He
wanted to hear the melody with brass instruments,
with reeds, and most recordings of the song used
strings. He wanted to hear strength and vigor. He experimented with the recording sphere, humming into
it, imagining how the song would sound with a driving
brass section, in full cry in an orchestra without strings.
The sphere played his fantasy back to him. Glorious
sound filled the room.

"So, I am John of Selbelle, arranger of popular songs."

Hell, that wasn't all bad. He could have some fun. He choose another sphere and recorded another of his favorites using woodwinds and flutes in addition to the brass and reeds. He ordered the sphere to play his creation but it was not his own music that came to his ears. It began so softly that it was felt rather than heard and then it swelled into a massed voice of instruments that were unfamiliar but utterly sweet. The sound expanded and a galaxy exploded into the rhythm of the stars and the flight of pulsars boomed from deep and distant voids. He could not move. He had never heard such glory.

He called out to One Alone and the Far Seer listened with him. Neither of them had the will to call a halt to the music, for it was the spirit of the universe captured with a thousand voices. When, at last, there was silence, when magnificence had faded and was gone, John whispered, "The balls are coded by color. The multicolored ones are thought recorders. Blue is for music. There are other colors."

"Quickly," One Alone said, and John understood. He began to sample different colored spheres. Light music was denoted by one color, music of infinite sadness by another. Now and then they would be mutually lost in some riveting work. John would shake his head to dispel the mood and move on to another sphere. There was music like fireworks. And then they heard the voice of the dead as a woman crooned sounds without words that sent John's blood pounding into erectile tissue. It was a call to ecstasy. He began to moan and writhe in need before One Alone interceded. John fell back onto his pillows, perspiration breaking out on his forehead.

"Wow," he said.

One Alone waited.

"It seems that all of these spheres are blanks or have music recorded on them," John said, feeling a bit ashamed that he had been so aroused by the voice of the female. He went into another room, found more music spheres and a few multihued blanks. When he found a different color, a brilliant red, he said to One Alone, "Well, here goes."

A voice came directly into his mind. There was no problem with language, for the images were created brain to brain. The voice had tone, timbre, expression. One Alone, present by invitation, was reminded of the language of Old Earth for each mental picture contained masses of information. It was a very sophisticated language; some words had multiple meanings.

"I dined with (the voluptuous female of the long, striking legs)," a male voice was saying. No name was used. The image was of a lovely woman.

"It seems to be a journal," John said.

There followed a long list of food that had been consumed during the dinner with the voluptuous female. As the foods were named, John could taste them and smell their aromas.

"Our agreement was to—" The image was not intended to be coarse or erotic, only factual. "—have union while under the influence of—" A drug.

John felt his heart sink. At last he had been able to break through, to reach into the past to hear the voice of one of the godlike tall ones and he was being subjected to a petty recounting of a sexual frolic. He started to turn off the communications, but One Alone said, "No, wait."

The tall ones undressed. John shared the emotions of the male, felt himself become erect again. He knew the smooth and lush body of a supremely beautiful woman. The experience left him weak.

"So now I can do my paper on the sex habits of a vanished race," he said to One Alone.

"It was all so shallow," One Alone said in amazement. "There was no hint of purpose or of anything outside the bedroom."

"You felt?" John asked.

"Very much so," the Far Seer admitted dryly. "We have a lot to learn."

"There are thousands of spheres," John said. He giggled. "If they're all like this one, wow."

He worked into the night. There was no auroral activity. The others slept. The spheres, like the other treasures of the city, were of a sameness. The music was wonderful, but the thoughts recorded in the red spheres banal, sensual.

If having unlimited power and riches and leisure reduces one to the level of a sexual automation," he said to One Alone, "I think I'll pass."

Trivia. "I told her of the laughing eyes to limit her activity with my tall and strong one." Jealousy.

"I transported to the home planet for the festival of the suns," a male said, and for a moment both John and One Alone were interested. "The group sexual activity was phenomenal."

John spent the hours of early morning going from apartment to apartment, searching out the red spheres. He learned one new thing. There had been lower animals on the world. "I have experimented recently," said a female voice, "with form change. I found the sexual responses—" The picture was that of a doglike animal. "—to be vaguely entertaining."

Vanity. "She of the red taste criticized my colors. I spent an hour altering the manner of decoration in my suite to conform with the multiplexed golds of a sunrise."

Shallowness. Food. Sex. Comfort. Lists of newly created possession.

"These are the thoughts of children," John said.

"Rest," One Alone said.

"There is only one thing of worth here," John said. "The music. You can choose almost any music sphere at random and be shattered with the brilliance of it."

"It is time to rest."

"It's as if they are oblivious to all but sensual pleasure."

"There was one mention of traveling through space," One Alone said.

"Yes, to go to a gang bang," John said. "No self-examination, no mention of how they created things, not even that glorious music. I don't understand. Someone, somewhere, must have been able to stop thinking about food and sex long enough to compose the music."

He rested and in the morning light asked Stella to lift him to higher apartments in other buildings. At midmorning he found a sphere whose color combination was different. He became involved in make-believe, in a bedroom farce with a multiple member cast. It was, of course, an erotic plot. Embarrassed, he asked Stella to leave his mind, but she giggled and stayed. There was an element of plot that he had not encountered previously. It was erotic, but it told a story. One half-serious attempt at creative activity among hundreds of personal journals detailing assignations with members of the opposite sex.

He continued his search until exhaustion and disappointment sent him to find a bed. He slept far into the night. Once again the skies remained empty of auroral color.

CHAPTER TWENTY

The thoughts of One Alone the Far Seer into the mind of the Keeper, Dear Companion, on Day 10 Month 3 of the Paulus Dead Worlds Expedition. Note that one segment of this entry is duplicated in the log of the U.P. Yacht Paulus marked "Removal or deletion prohibited." The log entry reads as follows:

Logged: *One Alone the Far Seer*
               Safety Officer, Paulus *Expedition*
To: *Admiral R.F. Worthy, Commanding*
               X&A Headquarters
               Xanthos II

This blinkstat will notify you of the death of all members of the X&A Authorized Paulus Expedition to the Dead Worlds. You may recover the Yacht Paulus at Blink Beacon DW-889-F-334.

I, One Alone the Far Seer, born on Old Earth, urgently demand X&A fleet action to first break up and then disassemble, repeat, disassemble, all twenty of the planets known as the Dead Worlds.

I invoke the provisions of the agreement negotiated by Capt. Bradley J. Gore, Commanding U.P.X. Pharos, with

Red Earth the Far Seer. The Gore-Red Earth pact recognizes the autonomy of the race you call the Old Earthers and accords Old Earthers special status within the United Planets Confederation. I invoke in particular that provision which recognizes Far Seers as Guardians of Life. Under this authority I dictate total destruction of the sac planets. I hereby declare the Dead World planets to be an unanswerable threat to the continued existence of both branches of our race.

The total disassemblement of these planets is to be accomplished from space without landing personnel. The closest approach is to be the maximum effective range of planet busters and disassemblers.

I repeat. There will be no planetside investigation before the destruction of the sac planets is accomplished.

Following total disassemblement of the twenty planets a pre-keyed command will release from the mind of my Keeper, Dear Companion, whom you will find aboard Paulus in deep sleep, all records and information necessary to explain this order. End Message.

So, my Dear Companion, that is done in the event that my worst fears are realized. Eyeless as I am, I weep. My heart is heavy with doubt, but we have gone too far to stop the processes of change now.

Throughout history the energies of my race were devoted to the effort of maintaining life on Old Earth. We lived to insure the fragile continuation of life, but we were different from the lower orders of animal life that existed before the destruction for no other reason, it seems, than to perpetuate the species. Even as we struggled to survive marginal living conditions, we were not indolent in other matters. We never lost our curiosity. Healers roamed the blasted countryside seeking scraps of knowledge. They knew and appreciated beauty. Far Seers studied the heavens beyond the poisoned atmosphere. Power Givers were our collective soul, and our mothers, contributing new life to the race.

The Old Ones, our ancestors, went into space not only to find living room or to gain relief from overpopulation and the threat of annihilation. There were other motives. Some sought more freedom. Others wanted land and material possessions, but there were those who wanted nothing more than the feeling of achievement and the satisfaction of knowing what lay beyond the stars.

Man has always been willing to endure danger and hardship in an effort to achieve his aspirations. Modern man tames hostile worlds in order to benefit financially from their resources, but also to make land and homes available to many. He sends his exploration ships into the vastness of the empty reaches not only for the worth of new worlds, but to expand his knowledge.

To make myself clear to those who may examine these thoughts at some future date, I do not seek material possessions. I do not seek power. My motive is the gathering of knowledge and, ultimately, to use this knowledge and the power that can be exercised by the members of this expedition to advance the welfare of the entire race.

All of which brings up questions. What is the goal of the human race? Is our destiny simply to people the life zone planets of this galaxy with our teeming billions?

Should our goal be to provide comfort and wealth to all? If so, we must believe that people of DW-3, at least, and probably of all the Dead Worlds, reached the pinnacle of civilization, for there was no hunger, no illness, no need, perhaps not even death on this world.

I pray to nature that I am not making a mistake that will eventually turn humanity into a race steeped in sloth and given to self-indulgence like those who once lived here. My young friends assure me that will not happen. They urge me to expose myself to the strongest of the auroral storms and join them in what they call a totally new awareness.

I am tempted, although I don't need superpowers to be able to celebrate life. I have no need for items of luxury. I am mesmerized with the idea of exposure not for myself, but for you, Dear Companion. I know that this is contrary to logic, for you, in your small existence, do not miss the things of sentient life because you know them not. It is selfishness on my part to think of you as being more than a Keeper.

If, indeed, you were changed by the effects of the aurora, I would be responsible for the alteration of nature's master plan, the plan that allowed our race to survive thousands of terrible years on a planet where conditions for life were marginal. Can I bring myself to do that?

The changes are evident in all of them now. They came late to Stella and Clear Thought, who were protected from the effects by their biological armor. I can't blame them for deviating from our purpose. Each of them has been given a new life and they are young.

I have not given up hope that they will be more practical once the novelty of being all-powerful has faded.

In my dreams I see a race of beings capable of traveling the entire universe to wring from it all of its secrets. I dream of participating in the exploration and that, I suspect, is my vanity, my weakness. I admit that my desire to know was influential in my decision to allow exposure to the aurora.

In that mixture of myth and recorded fact that makes up the history of our twin-branched race there is a quote from antiquity cited in the partially destroyed Book Of Rose The Healer. "Whom the gods would destroy they first make mad."

The humanoid race which peopled these worlds 75,000 N.Y. ago received what was probably their second or third exposure to the full strength of the aurora. I theorize that at least three aurora-producing conjunctions were required to lift life from humble beginnings to physical perfection as we know it. There is no empirical evidence to support my conjectures, but I propose that the ultimate rise of intelligence which terminated in moral rot happened within a period of a very few years following the auroral displays of 75,000 N.Y. ago. If I am right in my reconstruction of events, Dead World man had built an early industrial society perhaps two millennia prior to the last conjunction, utilizing fossil fuel. At the time of the third exposure of life on these worlds to the aurora the humanoids were less advanced than were my friends who have been so recently exposed. It took years after exposure, perhaps decades, for the Dead World race to develop omnificence. The changes in modern man have proven to be almost instantaneous.

I try to observe from a universal stance, not just from the viewpoint of a Far Seer. This much is in my favor as an impartial observer. I know what the Old Ones sometimes sneeringly call the pleasures of the flesh. Far Seers, perhaps as a reward for having been denied eyes and ears, were given a sensual nature and a match for it in their Keepers. Thus I can understand carnal urges and I do not condemn the enjoyment of sensuality by those who are discovering it for the first time. In fact, I rejoice in the

*blending of my fellow Old Earthers, and I can under-
stand the enthusiasm of my scaleless friends; but for the
first time in history the repeated blendings of Power Giver
and Healer do not produce offspring. Their blending is by
choice, in the manner of the Old Ones and the former inhabitants of these worlds, and is, again by choice, sterile.*

*This, however, is not the most important consideration.
It is the rapid and disturbing changes in basic attitudes
that disturb me most. For example, at first I reveled in the
joy of creating with the young artist from Selbelle III.
Now, so quickly, he no longer finds pleasure in creating,
but spends his time in the quicksand of sensuality. There
is, and I think this is an apt phrase, a plethora of mastur-
bation of the senses among all of them.*

*Ah, well. I will give them time. Meantime, although
the thought spheres all give forth with the same triviali-
ties, I will continue my random sampling of spheres, even
though I am satiated with gourmandism, gossip, vanity,
jealousy, pettiness, and carnality.*

*I keep remembering one isolated thought that was al-
most lost in a vivid, and, I admit, a moving description of
a ceremony involving group activity in one of the pleasure
caverns. The speaker was male. He seemed to be a bit
sated. He said he was ready to go to his high place and
think. There was not only boredom in his voice but, I suspect, a touch of regret.*

*On this world there are few high places. We set up
camp first in the low mountains. There is rubble there,
and Cecile has reconstructed for me a few luxurious
manors, but the thought spheres there are much the same.
On DW-6 there are high mountains. It is a planet that
was tortured by major upheavals of its crust materials.
Peaks soar to very respectable heights. If the man who*

sought his high place was being literal, DW-6 might prove to be interesting.

My course of action is far from simple, however. To continue to seek knowledge alone puts me at a disadvantage. I am not mobile. My natural ability falls short of the powers now wielded by my friends. I am limited in my research. I cannot soar, nor can I re-create. When I request their help, my friends do not refuse, but I sense that they are not interested.

I will brood no longer. My Dear Companion hungers.

CHAPTER TWENTY-ONE

He was a perfectly functioning, self-repairing, handsome, immortal biological perfection. He lay on a silken couch and fondled a small, furry animal that had joined him on his mental order. The little creature looked like a cuddly bear. He materialized a fountain in the center of the room. Perfumed water scented the air. Soon fish were cavorting in the basin of the fountain.

The furry animal and the fish amused him and frustrated him for, try as he might, he could not make either of them live. They were artful imitations of life, powered by the energies of his mind, just as the trees that surrounded his palace were mere counterfeits of life.

In a moment of pique he ripped the teddy bear apart to reveal its biomechanical guts. He disassembled the fragments and sent them drifting away. He let the fish deactivate and sink slowly to the bottom of the pool before he erased the fountain.

He had always been healthy, and he had been in the vigor of his youth before the change, but he had never known anything to compare with his current feeling of well-being. There had never been a day of his life when he had not known some discomfort, some ache, some pain, however small. He had never realized how irritating and debilitating small things can be, a grain of sand in the eye, stuffiness of the sinus, excessive heat or cold, a bumped head, a scraped shin. Now he knew only glowing, radiant health and it would be that way forever. He would never have a headache. He would never feel grainy-eyed from lack of sleep or semi-comatose from too much of it. He would never have indigestion, never be nauseous from drinking too much, never have a cold. It made him want to whoop with joy.

Considering the advantages, being unable to create life was only a minor annoyance. Perhaps, in time, he would be able to make a puppy. Certainly, when the time was right, he could father a child. He and his partner could choose the sex of the child. They could choose one particular sperm to fertilize a selected egg and tailor the child to the highest potential of their combined gene pools. If the child did not inherit omnificence genetically, he could alter its brain himself. By being able to examine and know his own body down to the level of individual cells, by being able to alter and heal and improve, he could apply that knowledge to the brain and body of another, his child, for example.

It was odd to think that for ages the race of man had used only an infinitesimal fraction of the potential of the human brain, but the truth had been before them all the time in the only book that had survived the voyage of the settlers from Old Earth. The Bible said that man was created in the image of God. True. Man had never believed. God could work miracles and man, in his image, could do the same if only he had enough faith; but it had taken an accident—the *Paulus* being in the sac system at just the right moment out of 75,000 N.Y., for the anciently predicted destiny of mankind to be realized.

He was godlike. If God wanted to keep the final god-like ability, the creation of life, for himself, that was all right. He rose, stretched, saw his form mirrored. He had made himself tall, an even seven feet. He had kept his own face while smoothing and perfecting his individual features. He was LaConius of Tigian, and proud of it.

He caught a musky, exciting hint of perfume and turned to see Cecile. She was no longer withdrawn. Her moods, during the early days of her transformation, were nothing more than frustration at being only partially complete. She had been able to sense perfection but not to reach it.

She was radiant. She was perfect in form. She was holding a bowl of sweet, ripe fruit. Cecile was still the most accomplished one of them when it came to forming edibles. She gathered atoms from the environment and made delicious things. It was not important that the seeds in the fruits she had assembled were, according to tests run by One Alone, sterile.

LaConius and Cecile had developed a relaxed but highly erotic relationship. He nibbled at an apple. She activated a music sphere.

"Sooner or later," LaConius said, "we're going to have to stop lollygagging around and get on with it."

"We have an eternity," Cecile said. "Time is no problem now."

"Yeah," LaConius said. "I guess you're right."

"Relax," she said. "Enjoy. We could spend years just listening to the music spheres."

"I'm thinking of going to Tigian." He was speaking aloud. Perhaps it was just habit, but he liked to hear his own voice, and he loved listening to the sweet, pleasant voice of the beautiful, tall woman who was his companion.

"Cone, are you still suffering from juvenile ambitions?"

"I have a duty to my family."

"You have nothing to prove. You're the greatest Iboni ever."

"True," he said, with a smile. "But someone has to watch the store. I was wondering if I shouldn't go back, put a quick fix on my younger brother—"

"Are you sure you're ready to have another one like us?" she asked.

"Just a partial fix. Just enough to make him a financial genius."

"There's time," she said, stretching in a feline way, causing her breasts to point against her silken blouse.

"Ummm," he said.

John and Martha were star jaunting. Reduced to pure thought, they roamed the void, sensing the incredible mass of the core, flitting through claustrophobic density as they entered the gravity well of the central blackness among stars more densely packed than anywhere else in the galaxy. John experienced the physical poetry of hydrogen fusion not for knowledge but for the experience, for the feel of it. He watched with some concern as Martha expanded her force-form and toyed with a sun, as the man in the bas-relief in the cave had done. She held the stuff of the universe in the palm of her hand, a sun twice the size of the local star of Terra II. After some experimentation she could toss the fiery orb from hand to hand like a ball while using the force of her mind to keep the movement from causing chaos among the nearby stars.

Tiring of the stars, they returned to DW-3 to find that LaConius had, after all, made a quick trip to his home planet. He spoke of soaring over his world on the wings of thought force.

"They are ants," he said sadly. "The world crawled with ants, working, striving, mewling, ants who are envious of their betters."

"And your family?" Martha asked.

"I don't know," LaConius said. "Somehow it didn't seem to matter."

Clear Thought and Stella, having at last satiated their fierce desire, visited Old Earth and were saddened. Terraforming was, for mere men, a young science and the effort of U.P. scientists to revive the murky, poisonous atmosphere of Earth was slow and expensive. Clear Thought and Stella could have purified the air and the oceans within hours, but they decided that it was not yet time to reveal themselves.

The two Old Earthers returned to DW-3 on a beautiful day in the endless October of a climate that they had all fashioned. They gathered atop a high building in a fine ballroom to share experiences. When the conversation moved toward an old question, what to do with their superhuman abilities, John said, "We're still limited, you know."

"Only by imagination," Cecile said.

"If you know it all," John said, "show me a picture of what was here before the big bang."

"Who cares?" Martha asked. "It doesn't really matter."

"Perhaps it is good that we are limited," Clear Thought said. "I for one wouldn't want to be able, for example, to cause the universe to quit expanding and begin to draw back toward the point of origination."

"I know what you mean," Stella said.

"I'm not sure I'm that limited," Cecile said. "I believe I could affect at least nearby galaxies."

"I hope that you don't try," One Alone said.

It was easy for all of them to forget that the Far Seer continued to hover over them up there aboard the *Paulus*, too hidebound or too frightened to join them in exposure to the strongest flowerings of color that were still to come.

"I hope that you will all come to care again about things that matter," One Alone said. "Are you not tired yet of your play and your toys?"

"There's time," Cecile said.

"Look around you," the Far Seer said. "You live with the luxuries of others, with the possessions of the dead. The waving of the leaves on the trees in the park below you are nothing more than a slight electrical current that is generated continuously in a small area of LaConius' brain. They are not real. You are living an illusion. There is no life around you, only reminders of death."

"When a sparrow has said peep, it thinks it has said everything there is to say," LaConius said, winking.

"Why is it that when you want to voice wisdom you

seek a quote from the Old Ones?" One Alone asked. "Have you no original thoughts of your own, LaConius?"

"I have felt the inner power of a star," Martha said. "When you can share this feeling, then maybe you can communicate with us on an intelligent basis."

"Am I no longer your friend?" One Alone asked.

"Of course," Stella said quickly.

"Martha?" the Far Seer asked.

"Yes," she said.

"Does that count for nothing with one who can play with a star?"

"Of course it does, old darling," Martha said.

Stella spoke. "We need your wisdom, One Alone. We miss your companionship. The aurora is building even now. Open yourself to it. Then you will be equal, perhaps more than equal, since your own natural abilities will be enhanced. Then you will be able to understand our thinking."

"Then will I join you in dancing a jig of ceaseless sensuality?"

"What you do would be your own choice," Cecile said, with ill-concealed anger.

"I feel your displeasure," Clear Thought said. "It's is true that we have been self-indulgent, but we have time. We're experiencing things that have been denied to us in the past. What do a few days matter?"

"Or a few years? Or a few decades?"

"Or a hundred years," LaConius said.

Stella sensed fear in the mind of the Far Seer. She spoke to him in private. "We offer no threat to you or to the race."

"In fact," he said, "you offer nothing. Where is your former high resolve to help all of mankind?"

Stella didn't answer.

Martha said, "The aurora will soon reach its peak and then it will fade away for 75,000 N.Y. You have only a little time, One Alone."

"Unless we decide to back things up and start the conjunction all over again," Cecile said, laughing.

Martha was intrigued. "That would take some doing," she said. She envisioned the sac system and its relationship to the galaxy. "Everything's interlaced. We'd have to affect the whole galaxy, and then it might not work. It just might be that the pull of a galaxy billions of light-years away is a part of the conjunction."

"It might be," One Alone said, "that someone tried to do just that once before."

Martha shuddered in spite of herself, for she was as much aware as any of them that they were not the first to enjoy perfection, not the first to know the secrets of power. Others had gone before them and they were dead.

"I would think," One Alone said, "that some very interesting things would happen if one began to alter the shape of the galaxy."

"I was just speculating," Martha said.

'Join us, One Alone," Stella urged. "We want knowledge, just as you want it. We would welcome your guidance."

"Then help me now, while there's still time to find out why twenty worlds were destroyed," the Far Seer said.

"What do you want us to do?" Clear Thought asked.

"Explore, investigate, read the thought spheres, journey to the other worlds and dig into the past until we know."

"Why not?" LaConius said. "I did find something different, One Alone. Remember when someone ran into that sphere in which a woman experimented with taking on the form of an animal?"

"That's just too depraved," Stella said.

"I wish they hadn't killed off the lower life-forms," John said.

"We don't know that there were other life-forms," Cecile said. "I haven't traced things back, but I wonder if the aurora didn't work on some primitive spore to advance evolution at a tremendous pace so that there was just one life-form."

One Alone listened sadly. Each time he tried to direct a sensible discussion, the others wandered off the subject, ignoring him.

"I just told you I found another sphere talking about becoming a lower animal," LaConius said.

"It's an intriguing idea, Cone," Cecile said. "I've always admired the Degland tiger. It's a really splendid animal.

"Show me," LaConius said with a grin.

Cecile showed him. A large, sleek, golden animal prowled the room on soft pads, rumbling softly in her throat. The animal looked back over her shoulder as she exited the room. LaConius cleared his throat and looked around at the others.

"Kiddies," he said, "I think it's time to feed the animal."

He patterned himself after Cecile's form as he entered a suite of rooms where the female tiger stood, lashing her tail, emitting the gut-wrenching aroma of estrus. It was a long and interesting night.

CHAPTER TWENTY-TWO

Since the personality of a Far Seer was invariably stable, for One Alone to indulge in a bit of frivolity was not weakness or deviation from purpose. There was time. He formed light-detecting organs and quickly discovered that the sense of sight was not as primitive as he had believed. His first view of the universe which, in the past, had been nothing more than echoes of his probing senses, was a writhing sea of color. The aurora was reaching its peak, having spread from the planet of its origin to engulf all twenty of the life zone worlds in the sac. The impact of the colors left him dazed.

He monitored the changes in his cerebral pattern as they happened. He had brought *Paulus* down into atmosphere and was standing in the open lock. He was able to re-form his eyeless dome after less than five minutes of exposure. As he watched the richness of a billion rainbows bathe the land below him, he felt infinitesimal electrical convulsions in his cerebral cortex. An awareness that was awe-inspiring grew in him. It had strained the senses of a Far Seer to detect the Earth's moon. Now one Far Seer could sense stars and bodies at galactic distances.

When the aurora faded, he indulged himself. Far

Seers had always been compulsive observers and collectors of data. He filled in blanks in his knowledge for several hours, but finally was forced to halt that rewarding activity. The six members of the expedition who were on the surface of the planet were together, deep in conversation. One Alone checked the ship, set the automatics after lifting her back into orbit, and allowed himself to become lost in thought. He could move his bulk without strain. He was fully mobile. He went to Dear Companion and saw her with his newly formed eyes. She was sweet and soft and helpless.

He made an alteration in his previously formed contingency resolution. If it should become necessary for him to terminate the experiment he would not, as he had stated in the message to be delivered to X&A, leave her alone aboard *Paulus*. There would be risk in that, for if an X&A ship were late in arriving she would die. Her brain was devoted to the storage of the lore of the race. In her infantile state she was helpless. If it became necessary for him to die, he would first provide for her future. He had the ability to do that now.

He monitored the conversations of his companions.

Stella was saying, not for the first time, "I think it's time we gave some thought to where we go from here."

"I'm a bit tired of artificial flowers," Martha said idly.

"Let's find a marginal world and terraform it," Clear Thought said. "Where life already has a beginning, we can alter it. I believe that I could start with a noxious weed and in a short while transform it into a useful, fruit bearing plant."

"That sounds like a long-term project to me," Martha said.

"We could go home and offer our services to the U.P.

council," Stella said. "I would like to work on Old Earth."

LaConius snorted in disgust. "You people are hung up on the small stuff," he said. "There are more serious matters to decide. For example, we can alter others to be like us. Now that's pretty damned serious, and I think we need to reach some agreement about it. We don't want one of us handing the power to some psychopath. How do you feel about making a pact to keep it to ourselves?"

"There are worthy arguments on both sides of the question," Clear Thought said. "The risks of making the change available to all are frightening, but to limit the gift to a few selected individuals would create an eternal dictatorship of the elite."

"There are still those who feel that benevolent and enlightened dictatorship is the most practical form of government," Cecile said. She laughed. "Not that I want to waste my time worrying about the population of a world."

"We could go away," Martha said. "We could find a nice little world so far from the U.P. that it would be centuries before the X&A ships could find it. We could pattern it to our own needs. I'm a little tired of living with the rather extravagant tastes of the tall ones."

John had not been listening. He was thinking of doing a heroic sculpture. His mind was searching the landscape for a rock scarp of the right size.

"There's something we keep ignoring," LaConius said. "One Alone."

"I've been thinking about him," Cecile said. "Since he won't join us, it might be a good idea to purge his mind of all knowledge of what has happened and send him home on *Paulus* with an implanted memory of our all being killed."

"You can't do that," Stella said, shocked.

"There're going to be one or two more flares," Clear Thought said, "and then it's over for 75,000 N.Y. If One Alone doesn't expose himself, we need have no fear of him."

"I don't know," LaConius said doubtfully.

"I think Clear Thought is right," Martha said. "He can't hurt us. We'll be around 75,000 N.Y. from now when the conjunction comes again and by that time maybe the race will be ready for it."

"I'm afraid that the race as a whole will never be worthy of the aurora," LaConius said. "Billions of people who would be able to drag a star into your lap and detonate it? No way."

"The more I think about it," Martha said, "the more I like the idea of an isolated world. It doesn't even have to be in this galaxy. Maybe that's what happened before. Maybe the people didn't die. Maybe they went far away."

"Afraid of what they might become after the next conjunction?" Stella suggested.

"We could build our own race," Martha said.

LaConius shook his head. "What if our children were born with the power? Could you trust a five-year-old who had the ability to play ball with a star? What if the little darling had a temper tantrum and exploded Mommy into individual atoms?"

"What if, a couple of generations later, one of our offspring develops a dictator complex?" Clear Thought asked.

"Simple," LaConius said. "Hail, Emperor of the Universe." He grinned. "That has a ring to it. Hail, LaConius, Exalted Ruler of this and all other galaxies."

"The tall ones had no government," Clear Thought said.

"After a few thousand years I might decide to give my subjects a break," LaConius said, waving his hand grandly. "I might give them the right to vote. For me only, of course."

"Oh, hush, Cone," Cecile said.

"Careful," LaConius said, "I'm not bored with you—yet."

Cecile's green eyes narrowed. "You are not indispensable."

"No?" He grinned. "If I don't ring your chimes, doll, who will?"

Cecile stepped back.

One Alone was on the point of intervening, but he was too late. He decided not to reveal himself, although he was revolted to the core.

A man in the uniform of the space service materialized. His eyes went wide and he crouched. "What the hell?" he asked, his voice shaking.

"Don't be afraid, little one," Cecile said. "You are dreaming. When you awake, you will be back aboard your ship and you won't even remember this lovely dream."

"You have got to be kidding," LaConius said. "You're going to try to substitute this midget for me?"

Cecile willed the man to grow. His uniform expanded with him. His eyes took on a look of panic and Cecile went into his mind to soothe him and to instil erotic desire.

"Well, two can play at that game," LaConius said. He

sent his mind searching, brought a young girl from Xanthos II. She screamed until he calmed her.

The disregard for the rights and lives of two human beings sickened One Alone. He went back into the aurora when it burst across the sac once more and stayed to the last, absorbing its odd force. His worst fears were being realized. He was saddened beyond sadness and there was nothing in the future except more tragedy. He found himself in violation of the most basic tenet of his being. He was anticipating his own death. That seemed to be the only answer. First he would be forced to go against a lifetime of reverence for life and then not even a Far Seer could be allowed to live while he held a power that could threaten the entire race. Soon he would take his last breath, but not before all of the others were dead, not before the twenty worlds of the sac had been pulverized into dust to be spread through the void. There would never be another conjunction.

He erased the message that he had left in the ship's log and sat beside Dear Companion's rack to make his plans. First he needed effortless mobility. He formed himself into a tall one. He created an image of the *Paulus* and left it behind as he thought the ship away, not bothering to activate the blink drive. In his absence the image of the ship would satisfy the others unless they examined it closely.

With *Paulus* orbiting another world of high mountains he began to explore the patterns of destroyed buildings. As on DW-3 there were great riches. His interest was in the thought spheres and to his relief he discovered that there was a vast difference in the spheres found in isolated dwelling places in the high mountains. In the first building that he reconstructed he found spheres of a composer of music. He began to reassemble dwellings and to examine thought spheres as swiftly as he could. He berated himself for not having changed sooner so that he would have had more time to find the answers.

He heard the thoughts of self-described scientists and realized with a grim smile that many of their speculations were childlike. The tall ones could feel and understand what happened in the nuclear furnace of a star. They could explore the galaxy, but they had little understanding of most elemental laws of physics.

Nevertheless, it was promising to find that not all of the tall ones had spent their lives seeking pleasure. He found one sphere dealing with the ultimate goals of the race and, although the work came from a rather childish mind, it proved that at least one man had been concerned about the future.

While One Alone worked on DW-6 the last flare of color filled the sac and faded with a finality that told him the aurora had ended. He was contemplating the contents of other spheres found in the mountain retreats. He no longer felt a sense of urgency. He checked on his former friends and companions. They had reached out to bring more humans to them. They had altered the bodies of the new ones to conform to their new standards of beauty. He told himself that he would do something soon. He could not allow people to be ripped away from their homes to be used as sexual pets.

He did not know as yet how the destruction of worlds came about, but he considered the actions of his former friends to be symbolic of the corruption that must have been a factor. In transporting human beings for their own pleasure without giving thought to the consequences, they were confessing their shallowness and their weakness.

He redoubled his efforts to ferret out the cause and manner of the destruction. He found half-baked philosophy, elementary science, interesting but shallow writings of fiction, lots of music, a few plays, and a four-dimensional game that taxed his mind. He had no need for rest. He could administer to Dear Companion's needs from a distance.

He found the imprint in time of a cleverly constructed retreat on the face of a vertical cliff hundreds of feet high. He noticed first the remnants of metal supports far back in the native rock. The dwelling had been cantilevered over the sheer drop. The pulverized rubble of its remains lay below at the foot of the precipice. He lifted the dust and put it back together. At first there appeared to be a disappointing sameness of content, but on second look he saw that there were fewer pieces of artwork, less clutter. The view was spectacular, and the rooms pleasant. The artifacts were tastefully arranged, the work, he felt, of an orderly mind. The thought spheres, instead of being scattered haphazardly, were stored in a specially constructed container on one wall. On another wall was a mobile model of the sac system showing the positions of all bodies during conjunction.

The thought spheres were numbered and indexed. He resisted the temptation to jump directly to the sphere that was the last entry in the index and began to read. The mind he discovered was different from all those he had encountered previously. Through the

thoughts of a being who had been gone for 75,000 N.Y.
he saw the sac system as viewed from space. It was a
masterful and exact creation. The vantage point shifted
slowly. The sac dwindled with distance to become lost
in the overall glow of the core.

One Alone placed the vantage point precisely as it
moved past the area occupied by the outermost worlds
of the United Planets Confederation and onward until
he was outside the galaxy. He saw the Milky Way edge
on. The central core bulged upward and downward.
The scene rotated and he saw the flattened disk of the
galaxy, an awesome sight.

With a swiftness that left him dizzy, the Milky Way
receded. He felt a great hunger to experience extraga-
lactic space for himself, not vicariously through the
eyes of another. The Milky Way merged with other galaxies and was nothing more than a mote among other
motes. Motion ceased. To that moment the sphere had
given him only visual data. A voice came to him.

"I could go farther, friend, but this example will suf-
fice. Our island universe, our galaxy, is only one among
many. We must remember this and ask ourselves, 'Can
we be alone in such a vastness?'"

For the first time One Alone felt something akin to ad-
miration for a tall one. This mind had been working toward a realization of the unity of all life. This dead one
was speculating, as man, himself, had done so often,
about the whys. This one was, like man—who, in spite
of all his exploration and questioning, was still alone—
feeling isolation. This mind would have understood the
Far Seers' sense of brotherhood with all life, for this tall
one was a seeker. The urge that had sent X&A ships
probing outward was not exclusive to man. Life sought

life. The same drive that had sent Bradley J. Gore to the Earth's moon to meet Rack the Healer at the time of death had been felt 75,000 N.Y. in the past by the mind of one who was long dead.

To feel kinship with at least one tall one was disturbing to One Alone, for it required a reassessment of his thinking. He shook his head, compared, found the fallacy in comparison. Man wanted to know whether or not he was an isolated oddity, an aberration in an otherwise insentient universe, but he searched somewhat humbly and with no little fear. The mind that could negate intergalactic distances had no doubts that it was the most intelligent thing in the universe.

Man the seeker had encountered not other intelligent entities, but evidence that such beings had existed. He found the charred worlds of the vanished Artounee and the preserved record of the death of that race along with their conquerors, the Delanians. And he found the Dead Worlds. He saw destruction that made him cautious and underlined his latent fears of the dark, but did not cause him to abandon his search. Perhaps he sought reassurance that he was not evil. Perhaps he hoped that somewhere there existed a race whose purity and goodness would tell him that he, himself, was at least partially good.

Man's reward, One Alone promised, would not be to become toys for a handful of artificially created supermen who could destroy worlds.

He returned to the sphere and the thoughts of the wise one who had traveled into deep space to wonder. As he listened and experienced, he tried to place the time of the long trip, to relate it to the time scale of the U.P. By studying the positions of stars he determined that while the mind of the tall one was traveling outside the galaxy the first small colony of Old Ones on Terra II was struggling up from enforced primitivism, trying to lift themselves back into space with the task of building a technology ahead of them.

Evidently, the tall ones had not encountered man either on Old Earth or on Terra II. The galaxy was vast, even for one who could travel with the speed of thought. The tall one who had viewed the galaxy as one tiny mote among billions might have said, upon encountering man, "Hail, brother, let us work together."

Or, One Alone thought grimly, he might have found the daughters of man to be fair and taken them to his bed.

Hurriedly he studied the spheres, looking for more clues to the mind that had fed them. He wanted to know how the tall one looked, wanted to be able to define his personality, wanted, more than anything else, to find proof that at least one of the tall ones had believed in good.

One Alone had always believed that Nature protected life. His faith had been sorely tested on the Dead Worlds. He was not sure whether it had been accident or Nature that prevented the discovery of man on his two small worlds by the tall ones. Was it divine providence or coincidence that had prevented man from becoming toys for the tall ones, perhaps to perish with them? Had Nature experimented with perfection on the Dead Worlds and, seeing the mistake, brought down terminal punishment? Whatever the reason, man had been saved by the death of billions of beautiful people.

He lifted his head and shouted aloud. "I will not allow my faith to be destroyed."

Nature protected life. When the Old Ones seared Earth with nuclear fire, Nature continued life in the form of the New Ones—Seer, Keeper, Healer, Power Giver. When Earth seemed intent on wiping out all life except noxious, low-level vegetation, Nature brought Old Ones back to the original home to save Earth's people.

Life, some cynics said, was an accident, and not necessarily a lucky accident. If one believed that, the meeting between Bradley Gore and Rack the Healer on Earth's moon was nothing more than coincidence just as the first union of amino acids and the energy of the sun was a random chemical reaction. One Alone could not accept this. The universe itself didn't care, for it was cold and impersonal, and hostile to life except in rare oases, but somewhere there was a divine power. Somewhere Nature lived, and cared, and intervened now and then in times of dire emergency.

His suspicion that Nature had protected man from discovery by the tall ones was reinforced by another sphere on which the tall one recorded an account of a trip that took him to within a few light-years of a small star that One Alone identified as Earth's sun.

The next sphere he studied was a surprise. A female voice commented on the same subjects that had been covered by the male. Up to that time One Alone had assumed that the orderly establishment that clung to the side of a cliff was the home of the male, but as he listened further he learned that the male was a correspondent of the female who had build the orderly retreat. As the day went on, he discerned that the female had been in contact with dozens of thinkers in various fields. For some time he was bogged down in the cursory speculations of self-styled scientists. He checked several spheres, hoping for another from the wise space traveler.

His lagging interest was fired by a new voice contemplating the history of the sac race. In the beginning the tall ones lived on the bounty of the fruitful planet which One Alone called DW-19. He had been right in thinking that DW-19 was the home world. Life was sweet. There were animals to provide clothing and flesh for food. Tools were made of stone and communication was by vocalization. In short order machines were built to extract coal from the earth to provide warmth, power, and comfort. There was a written language. The rise of the technological society was slow.

With One Alone waiting eagerly, questions bubbling in his mind, the tall one went into a long analysis of the dead, oral language of the primitives. It was important information for a member of a race that knew of only two languages other than the picture language mental communication of the Old Earthers, but One Alone was impatient.

The female joined in the discussion of language. She theorized that, although there was no remnant of the written language of the ancients, communication could be achieved by physical renderings of thought images. The male said that her assumption presupposed a need to communicate with other intelligent beings who utilized radiant energy to gather information and could not exchange thoughts. The female said that any being who used light as data would translate an image of an eye to see, look, or observe.

One Alone's pulse quickened. There was such an image. It was carved deeply into the bedrock of DW-I, the first planet to be seen by a ship entering the sac system. The inscription began with the image of an eye. *Look on this, ye who aspire, and quake. Build not, for we shall return.*

The discussion between the female and the man who studied the dead, written language continued. One Alone's heart went cold when the female chose an example to explain how abstract images could be solidified with visual pictographs.

It would be impossible, the male maintained, to express in a simple symbol a concept that could not even be imagined by those who did not have the power of mind to alter the natural order of things. The female agreed that it would be difficult, but that it might be done by borrowing from the old, written language. To express an abstraction such as that being discussed it would have been necessary for the language makers to invent a new word, or perhaps make a union of two old words. The two words suggested by the female were create and ideate. They combined to form the word, creideate. The word expressed the ability to alter nature, to create with the force of the mind.

One Alone put the sphere aside. He knew that both the tall ones and those who had discovered the Dead World had failed. The tall ones had not expressed the abstraction well and man's translation was flawed because of the limitations of his understanding.

One Alone created paper and a writing instrument. With deep emotion he wrote down the correct translation of the inscription on DW-I. It took only a few seconds. For 15,000 N.Y. man had taken the inscription to be a threat when, actually, it was a warning.

He rewrote the warning, lengthening it to contain all the meaning that its originators had intended. He wrote it in the language of the Old Ones. He read it over and over.

"Well," he said aloud, his voice soft in the silence of an empty world, "you're a trusting fellow after all, man."

And just a bit self-centered. In his innocence, in his egotism, man had decided that the inscription had to be a threat directed toward him when, in fact, poor man, the tall ones had not even known of his existence. Only one of the tall ones—at least as far as One Alone could determine—had speculated about the possibility of other intelligent life. Only a few, perhaps one or two of the tall ones, had cared enough to carve the inscription in the bones of a dead world, and their warning had not been intended for space wanderers, but for home consumption. The warning had been carved after the death of but one world and it was intended for other tall ones.

See death around you, you who creideate, and desist. Tamper not with the fabric of reality or this destruction will be yours through your own doing.

He wished momentarily for someone with whom to share the irony. Billions of credits and mountains of materials had been expended by the human race since the discovery of the Dead Worlds to counter what they felt was the ultimate threat. A race had armed itself to be prepared for the promised return of the planet killers and all the while the event that caused a shiver of dream for all who saw the Dead Worlds had been an act of suicide, not of murder.

He returned to the spheres. He learned more about the race which mutated with deadly swiftness following the conjunction of 75,000 N.Y. past. They had been, truly, like infants who possessed omnificent power. Only a few of them, the thinkers in the high places, connected the leap past steam engine technology to effects of the aurora. Most had accepted the gifts as their due, just as One Alone's companions had. The race substituted creideation for industry and, suddenly ashamed of their past, erased all traces of industry and everything that would have reminded them that they had not always been gods. They spread on the wings of thought to the other planets of the system and bred with gusto. In the beginning there was idealism, so that marginal planets were made into paradises, but that burst of creativity gave way to the well documented search for sensual pleasure.

It happened in just over one thousand years. Only a few, among them the female of the cliff dwelling, took time from pleasure to question.

When a private quarrel devastated a planet, a corps of Watchers was formed from the ranks of the solitary thinkers of the high places to guard against repetition of the disaster. One Alone identified the planet as DW-5, and shook his head in ironic recognition of the distinction of a planet that had been denuded twice. The first destruction was the result of a lovers' quarrel.

The female of the cliffhouse was a Watcher. She recounted several malicious attempts at wholesale destruction and spoke of the weeding out and "neutralization" of several psychopathic personalities who posed danger for others. She spoke of punishment for pranks such as the premature detonation of an aged star by a young man who wanted to observe a super-nova. She recorded actions taken to prevent importation of water worlds to the sac system. She, like other Watchers, began to complain of the work load. It prevented them from living life as they chose. She said that constant awareness was required to police the thoughtless creideating of billions of idlers. Scientific inquiry was being stifled, since all those with more or less independent minds were engaged in control of the madness that was endemic in the general population.

On a lark, two young ones changed the course of two large galaxies to see the effects when suns collided. One Alone, on hearing this, wondered if the fate of the beautiful Artounee and the cruel Delanians had been determined, there within the colliding galaxies in Cygnus, by a childish escapade. He lost what little regard he had for the tall ones, thinking of the terrible irony of the frivolous destruction of the winged females of the Artounee by members of an idle and worthless society.

The wise space traveler cataloged other tamperings. In idle curiosity, a tall one, under the influence of a designer drug, tore the fabric of space and for a hectic moment the existence of the universe was threatened until the corps of Watchers repaired the damage after quickly snuffing out the existence of the perpetrator. A conference of Watchers was called. They gathered in a large mountain establishment. One Alone saw them as they were recorded by the mind of the orderly female. He knew a few of them from their correspondence with the female. He felt their sense of urgency, and even some fear.

They communicated in a babble of thought. They were determined to prevent more capricious experi-

THE OMNIFICENCE FACTOR 213

mentation. One Alone had to repeat sections of the proceedings in order to catch all of the intermeshed thoughts. They bemoaned how crisis followed crisis. They discussed the fecklessness of the race as a whole and regretted the loss of purpose in the society. They agreed about the problems of controlling twenty planets peopled by billions of childlike pleasure seekers each of whom had the power to destroy the universe.

A program of education for the masses was proposed. Individual voices spoke of more drastic measures. A hush fell over the gathering when it was proposed that the twenty worlds be "neutralized." It was as if that suggestion sobered them, for now the voices were easily distinguished.

"We cannot hope to continue to prevent serious events."

"We are helpless to control billions of children."

"But to neutralize all? Who will choose?"

"This body. This organization of Watchers."

"It would have to be done quickly and without warning."

"I doubt the ability of the group to accomplish the deed without some fear of retaliation."

"We can easily turn them against each other."

"That would mean total destruction."

"Which we can repair."

"Yes. Jealousy. Rivalry. Something as simple as an argument over the color scheme of an apartment can be fanned. A fight over a sexual partner. We can build on such things."

"Actually, we wouldn't have to delve so deeply to find a dispute that could be ignited. It would be child's play to plant the idea on one world that another is planning a peremptory strike."

"Can't we devise a method of neutralization that will leave the worlds undamaged?"

"Do you people realize that you are speaking of the murder of billions?"

"We speak of the continued existence of the universe. You were not present when one individual almost brought nothingness."

"Perhaps if we merely thinned the population with selective strikes."

"That would risk retaliation by the survivors."

"Is your life so important that it should not be risked to save the universe?"

"I favor setting world against world. We can pool our resources to protect a few sanctuaries and a basic stock of Watchers with which to repopulate the worlds."

"Why repopulate? We would merely be creating conditions for another slaughter."

"We can decide whether or not to reseed the worlds with proven stock at a later date."

"The proven stock being ourselves?"

"I know of no other possibility."

"I see billions dead."

"I see that our worlds are saved, not to mention the galaxy and the universe."

"Perhaps they will not cooperate in destroying themselves."

"They will."

"I think we should conduct a trial to see if our theory will work."

"On a small scale."

"Yes."

One Alone shivered. The gathering had dispersed at that point, each of the Watchers going back to his or her individual retreat. He had no way of knowing how much time had elapsed. He could not guess when the trial had begun. He was given a reference number to indicate the next thought sphere. He searched for it in the container. It started with a blast of thought in high excitement.

"Warning, warning, destructive force."

"The trial begins."

"Do we control now?"

"No. It is over."

"So quickly."

"Two worlds dead."

The speakers were well known to One Alone. They were the orderly female and the wise space traveler.

"So," the wise one said, "it is as we thought. They co-operated willingly in their eagerness to kill."

"I go now," the female said.

Was there regret in her thought voice?

"I, too, need some time for thought," the wise one said. "We will meet again."

With explosive incisiveness another mind penetrated and was recorded on the sphere. "Who?" demanded the wise one.

"Watchers!" the newcomer screamed. "Watchers. It was Watchers."

"They know," the wise one said, following a moment of silence.

"Watchers," the female called urgently, "strike, strike, strike. The madness spreads."

"They know why," the wise one said sadly.

"Watchers," the thoughts of the female screamed. "Now, before it is too late."

In a conference of minds formerly calm voices rose in fear and agitation. One Alone could decipher only scattered bits of information from total chaos. He knew that worlds were dying one by one. The Watchers had lost control. They had been discovered and the tall ones, having watched planets die, were striking out blindly in a futile effort to kill the killers.

The female said, "To space."

For the first time, through the eyes of the wise one, One Alone had a picture of the orderly female. The wise one thought of her as Long Hair.

"To space and quickly, Wise One. There is the only safety."

The sphere continued to be in communication with other Watchers.

"I weaken. Help me."

"I am under attack. Help me."

Long Hair's voice. "It's all rather magnificent, isn't it, Wise One?"

"Are you mad?"

"No more than you, my friend."

"The death of billions and the destruction of worlds is a magnificence?"

"Do you intend to survive?" Long Hair asked.

"I must fight to save—something."

"It is too late. Join me in space."

"I fight."

The babble of thoughts began to fade. There were cries for help and then silence.

One Alone felt weak. There were no monstrous planet killers poised to sweep down upon the United

Planets from distant space. There were no ogres. There had been only people, people much like man, himself. Billions of them had died in a chaos of pettiness. Thus it must have been in the last hours of nuclear terror as the Old Ones convulsed the crust of Old Earth and illuminated her atmosphere with the brilliance of a sun. They had fired their rockets to the very last, a terrible exercise in overkill, just as the tall ones had sent out their messages of havoc to the last.

"I must have faith," One Alone whispered to himself, but it was difficult. Was it the destiny of life to end as it had ended on Old Earth, on the planets of Cygnus, on the Dead Worlds? "Faith," he said. "It cannot be so."

He refused to give in to the darkness that threatened to engulf him. He fought against his depression, telling himself that even the Watchers had lacked nobility of purpose and that was their failing. There was purpose to life.

He returned to the *Paulus*, feeling a deep need to touch the soft flesh of his Dear Companion. She was in his arms before he remembered. The realization lanced through him.

At least one of the tall ones had survived. He pictured the female called Long Hair by the wise traveler. He could hear her voice in his mind.

"To space," she had said. "There only is safety."

Long Hair lived. Perhaps others had escaped as well to form a breeding unit, to travel far, even beyond the galaxy. Perhaps his thinking regarding the inscription on DW-I was wrong, after all. Perhaps it had been carved after the destruction and was a warning to man or any other intelligent race that reached the sac system. If the planet killers lived, if even one of them had survived, they, or she, could return.

A beautiful woman alone in space for almost 75,000 N.Y. Could any mind survive loneliness for so long? Was she near, the long-haired one, watching at the time of the aurora, ready to enforce the warning against creideation? He sent his expanded senses searching the emptiness. He felt nothing.

But it was good to lie beside his Dear Companion. He indulged himself. He had time. The most painful decision of all could be postponed for a little while.

CHAPTER TWENTY-THREE

"Good Evening. I'm Mark Jarrman and this is *Cosmos*, the program which delves into the story behind the headlines and introduces you to the personalities who made today's news. Our guest tonight is Professor Arthus Paulus of Xanthos University. Professor Paulus, as you know, is the foremost analyst of language. He is responsible for the official translation of the manuscripts brought home from the colliding galaxies in Cygnus and he is currently working closely with the Department of Exploration and Alien Search in a study of the emerging scraps of lost languages being discovered during the archaeological work being done on Old Earth.

"It is not for his expertise in linguistics that we have asked Professor Paulus to be with us tonight, however. As it happens, he was quite close to the six young people who have been listed as missing on an expedition to the Dead Worlds. He taught each of them in one or more of his classes and he participated in the planning of the expedition.

"Professor Paulus, the minority members of the Congress of the Confederation are calling for a significant expenditure of funds in an effort to, as they put it, solve the mystery of the Dead Worlds once and for all.

In your opinion, do recent developments, namely the loss of a space yacht with six people aboard, warrant still another expedition to the Dead World sac?"

"Mark, I am only a teacher."

"That's the understatement of the week. We all know that X&A came to you first when it was discovered that the inscription carved into the bedrock of DW-I had been altered."

"About that I can have an opinion. I do not consider myself to be qualified to comment on whether or not the Congress should appropriate money for another investigation of the Dead Worlds. I teach literature and language. I do not make statements on political matters. Of course, I would never begrudge money spent on legitimate scientific inquiry."

"Thank you, Professor. Let's put you to work in your own speciality. Do you feel that the meaning of the new inscription is quite clear?"

"Very clear."

"Which brings up an interesting question or two. Why was the inscription altered and who did it? Do you agree with those who say that it was done on a lark by the *Paulus* expedition?

"I do not."

"After all, they were young. Graduate students."

"They would not do such a thing as a prank."

"I assume that you base your opinion on what you know of the character of the six members of the expedition?"

"Yes."

"In your opinion, then, none of those aboard the yacht that was named for you had the distorted sense of humor or the lack of responsibility to change the inscription, not even for the sake of creating a conundrum inside the enigma of the Dead Worlds?"

"Each member of the expedition passed a screening by X&A. As you know, the sac system is closed to all but serious scientific investigation. Obtaining clearance to go there is not easy, and requires not only security but character clearance. X&A conducted careful psychoprobes of each individual before giving permission."

"Could you tell us about those who were aboard the *Paulus*?"

"LaConius Iboni, whose family financed the expedition, is the son of one of the first families of the Tigian system. It would be highly unlikely for such a young man to act irresponsibly or to allow others to do so. The Safety Officer of the expedition is a Far Seer who is known, of course, as a wise and honorable man."

"You use the present tense, professor. I take it that you think they may still be alive."

"I'm a creature of hope, Mark. I pray that they are alive for the sake of their families and for myself. I was quite fond of all of them."

"Professor, the X&A ship *Earthglow* was sent to check on the expedition when it became overdue. The *Earthglow* found no trace of either the *Paulus* or its passengers. The X&A investigators found plaques marking archaeological digs made by the *Paulus* expedition, so there was evidence that the missing persons did arrive and work at the Dead Worlds. The most puzzling finding of the *Earthglow*, however, was a breathable atmosphere on DW-3, a planet that, when last visited, had poisonous gases in lethal quantities."

"What can I say that hasn't been said?"

"Please tell us more about the members of the expedition."

"They were, as you have noted, young. They were good students, some better than others. Oddly enough, I first met them as a group in my alien literature class. They had become friends during their first year at the university. I had them in other courses later, usually as a group."

"Which of them stands out in your mind?"

"Each had his own personality. Each had potential. I have great respect for all of them. John, from Selbelle, was a dedicated artist. He had definite ambitions. He was a dreamer, but also a doer, as most artists are. He wanted to go back to Selbelle III, his home planet, to teach young artists until he became self-supporting. He—"

One day John looked out over the swaying tops of the artificial trees and saw his mountain. He climbed it to the top to slice away a peak, leaving a vertical surface of smooth stone, the largest canvas ever envisioned by an artist. It measured over one mile from side to side, half a mile in depth. It was there waiting for him and he knew exactly how the finished work would look.

He gazed at the smooth side of the mountain, then let his eyes shift down to Martha's sleeping face. Voices came to him from another room. Cecile was playing with her flesh and blood toys. For a moment he felt uneasy. He walked to the window and stared at his mountain. He soared away without waking Martha and began to work. First the flat surface had to be carved. Then he would highlight it in brilliant color. He felt a surge of elation as the first lines of the work began to emerge. He worked all day, ignoring Martha's calls. By late afternoon he was splashing red ores and the fire of jewels onto his work. The picture glowed. Had it been created on Selbelle III it would immediately be recognized as one of the wonders of the United Planets. People from all over the Confederation would travel to see it and to admire his genius.

It would be easy enough to have his work seen on Selbelle III. He could simply move the mountain into the desert near his home city. He was John, the artist, and an artist wants others to see his work.

He envisioned the reaction of his teachers, his family, his friends. He almost yielded to temptation, but he was reminded of how Cecile and LaConius were using imported men and women. He was uneasy about that. Martha had experimented with it, but she had quickly sent her pet back to his home planet with no memory of his experience. He decided not to move the mountain back to the U.P. because it would be exploitation of innocent people to expose them to such shock.

On the other hand, he thought, he was not being selfish in his desire to have others see and enjoy his work. He could bring selected people, perhaps even Professor Paulus, to his mountain, allow them to see it, and send them back with or without the memory of the work in their minds. By leaving the knowledge of the great work with them he would be enriching them, after all.

An artist works for his own satisfaction, of course, but he is not fulfilled unless his work means something to others. He was in a quandary. In the end he gave in and flew on wings of thought to the art colony near the

University on Xanthos where he randomly selected half a dozen people to accompany him. He placed them down in front of his mountain where they stood fearfully, gazing in awe at the miles-long panorama. It was at that moment, just as his guests were beginning to recover from their trauma and make comments on his work that he felt the first onslaught of force. His unconscious mind shouted a warning, but he was unprepared, for his eyes were filled with the beauty of his own work. He did not regret dying so much as being robbed of knowing the reaction of his guests to his art.

"No," he shouted as he lashed back with a strike of world-crushing force.

"Mark, they were all above average students. Clear Thought, the Old Earth Healer, had one of the most logical minds I've ever encountered. He would seek me out after class to engage me in discussion and his questions were incisive. He had the intellectual curiosity that is the mark of the Healer, a type known for curiosity. He wanted to know everything, from something simple—like what is over the next hill—to how the human brain functions."

"I understand, Professor Paulus, that Healers are actively recruited by X&A for exploration work because they adapt to the rigors of a long cruise easily and can function without space armor under marginal conditions. What are some of the other character traits of a Healer?

"Clear Thought loved life, and he shared that enthusiasm with everyone. His plans were to take his terminal degree as a result of the *Paulus* expedition and then to enlist in the space service. He knew what he wanted in life and was not reluctant to talk about it. His dream was to be a part of an X&A expedition that found intelligent life among the stars. He knew that he had some important decisions to make regarding the peculiar physiological relationship between Healers and Power Givers."

"I believe that they use the term coloration for their, ah, mating."

"Both male and female color on intimate portions of their bodies. That is nature's signal that they are ready for the act of propagation. This evolutionary adaptation is assumed to have come about to insure effective diversity among a small population. Clear Thought and Stella the Power Giver were close, but there was no guarantee that they would color at the same time under any circumstances, and Clear Thought's desire to join X&A made it highly likely that they would be separated before coloration came to them. There is no way to predict the process and no way to accelerate or delay it. His problem was that if he stayed with Stella he might waste years with the possibility that one of them would color alone."

"I read just this week, Professor Paulus, that X&A have taken the mating habits of the Old Earthers into consideration, that they now allow pairs to enlist and serve together on the same ship."

"A long overdue move. A Power Giver and a Healer make an excellent team. LaConius of Tigian knew that when he offered berths on his ship to Clear Thought and Stella."

"Professor, the members of the *Paulus* expedition were young and inexperienced, but they seemed to have been well organized. With a Far Seer and the other Old Earthers in the group, what could have happened to them?"

"Mark, all I can say is that ships have disappeared in deep space before and probably will again."

Clear Thought's sense of curiosity had been dulled by continued joy. Now and then he felt the pull of space. He had total access to endless parsecs of exploration, and that knowledge faded before—Stella. Their love no longer depended on the whims of nature.

He was aware that their dedication to each other was a source of amusement for his friends. At first, when they spent all their time alone exploring the most glorious aspect of their gift, the others teased. After the initial rush of getting to know the joys of merging they had, through form change, shared with the New Ones only to find that the most intense satisfaction came from each other, and that no casual sexual play came close to their own mergings. They withdrew from group activities.

Splendid as it was, luxurious beyond belief as it was to be able to blend with Stella whenever either of them was aroused, there came a day when the natural wanderlust of the Healer could not be denied. He ventured into the blackness of space on invisible force. He felt only emptiness and loneliness. He conducted a swift and boring exploration and returned to the heaven where he and Stella colored continuously.

"Cecile was born in Xanthos City. She was a bit more cosmopolitan than the others and yet she was innocent in her own way. She was a laughing girl, always ready with a quip. She was studying architecture, but she had so many interests that I sometimes wondered if she'd ever be able to concentrate on any one thing. She was determined to enjoy all aspects of life. It pleased her ego to make good grades, so she worked just hard enough to do so. She was surrounded by witty, intelligent, and pretty people, although her core group was composed of those who later made up the expedition. She was much in demand, and dated quite a number of eligible lads. I suppose her future would have been linked to Xanthos society, for she was one of the beautiful ones."

Cecile's bright hair brushed the face of a perfect male who had been fashioned to her tastes from a man transported from one of the U.P. planets. She had grown tired of living in the apartments and manors of the dead ones and had fashioned an establishment of her own. The decor was reminiscent of her home on Xanthos, with rich touches of Dead World splendor. She had chosen the colors to compliment her hair and her pale rose complexion.

She felt that John was wrong in criticizing her for using imported human pets. The dear little things had the time of their lives, even if they wouldn't remember any of it when she tired of them and sent them back. With them, there was at least a suggestion of variety and diversity. LaConius, for all of his big talk, was often boring.

With the altered human male she walked out onto balcony overlooking a lake. LaConius contacted her from his large house on the other shore.

"You're getting to be rather promiscuous, aren't you?" he asked.

"Delightfully so," she said, laughing.

"Want to have a group thing tonight?"

"Why not?" she asked. She sent the man off to have a nap until she needed him again. She left him sleeping when she transported herself to the house across the lake. Only LaConius and Martha were present. John was fooling around with his mountain again.

"We can bring in help," Martha said. "There is an X&A ship a few parsecs away and the captain is a nice-looking man."

Cecile smiled. "Don't pick the nicest one for yourself."

"What about me?" LaConius asked.

"There are women aboard," Martha said.

Cecile was searching for the ship to make her own choice when she felt the first pain. She was ready. Her reaction was instantaneous. She had altered first and had enjoyed the powers longer than the others. She had been expecting the attack. She lashed back with immense strength.

"The other human girl was Martha, right?"

"Martha of Terra II, Mark, but remember that all of the members were human."

"Sorry. No offense intended. It's just that it's so confusing to use the terms Old Ones and New Ones."

"Martha was a serious-minded girl, somewhat provincial when compared to Cecile, but of all of them perhaps the most dedicated to learning. She burned with a desire to make things better on old Terra II. She was an idealist. She showed signs of becoming a valuable member of society."

Martha felt only slightly guilty about taking part in another temporary abduction. She rationalized her action by saying that if John hadn't gone off to play with his mountain she wouldn't have been forced to call in outside help. Actually, she preferred being alone with John to the games that LaConius and Cecile liked to play.

Even as the evening's entertainment progressed, she could not overcome something that was becoming more and more bothersome. She was homesick. It was about time for her to tell the others that she was going home, that she was not going to wait any longer to cure the ills of Terra II.

She watched Cecile and LaConius as they entertained themselves with a male and a female crew member from the distant X&A ship and thought of her home, of her parents. She did not feel the first indication of attack. She reacted to Cecile's counterstrike.

"The driving spirit behind the expedition was LaConius of Tigian. He knew that his was a noble destiny. He was a tall young man, and quite handsome. He was a plodder, but he usually arrived at his intended destination. At odd times he showed flashes of brilliance in scientific fields. It was he who suggested a possible explanation of the Cygnus tragedy that interests scientists and scholars to this day. He was preparing himself to take his place in the family business and, I believe, for political activity as well. In my opinion he would have been a strong leader."

LaConius hoped that Cecile would soon tire of her repetitive games with the altered pygmies from the U.P.

She had been the most beautiful girl he'd ever met before the change and now she was nothing short of spellbinding. It didn't make him jealous for her to have a little fun with the imported toys. He enjoyed it himself sometimes, but of late there seemed to be a certain futility involved. He found himself thinking of the purple and red sunsets on his own world. He wanted to heard the songs of real, living birds. It was time to move on. He didn't have the concerns of One Alone about turning a superman loose in the U.P. He had enough common sense to control his appetite and keep his powers hidden until it was time to reveal himself.

He liked to envision a scene, starring LaConius of Tigian, where he would stand before the representatives of worlds and say, "I have come as the head of the Iboni family to relieve you of your fears and worries. I will take care of you."

If he wanted to, he could be even more specific, and anywhere in the galaxy where he chose to be ruler from Xanthos to the periphery. He could protect all, and lead the U.P. to a greatness which had not been imagined in the minds of the little ones.

"I will teach you," he would say to his old teachers. "I will unlock for you the secrets of the universe. In my youth I explained to you the quasi-stellar radio sources beyond Cygnus. Now nothing is hidden from me."

Well, pretty soon now. One of these days he'd travel out to Cygnus. He had always been intrigued by the story of Miaree and the Artounee. Maybe tomorrow.

The force hit him and he screamed as he mustered all the power of his mind.

* * *

"Stella the Power Giver was gentle, as are all of her kind. She was Earth Mother, considerate of all, giver of life to her race. I suspect that if she and Clear Thought had flowered together before the expedition left Xanthos she would have considered that gift enough for the moment and would have tried to improve her knowledge in some other way while tending her child."

"This time," Stella said, "I am going to allow conception. It is time. I will select the sperm that will become a Healer, like you."

"Why not a Power Giver with your eyes?" Clear Thought asked.

"At any rate, we will be three," she said. "I think then that it will be time to leave this place."

"And where will we go?"

"To offer our services to mankind, through X&A, I suspect."

There was no more talking. As the moment of conception neared she felt the slide of emotions, knew that her egg was ripe and waiting for its union with the male seed. It was glorious, more intense than any of the sterile mergings.

She screamed, "No, no," in loss and sadness. "Not now, One Alone, not now." Not just as she was about to know the ultimate experience. She couldn't believe that he was serious, but death danced toward her and she screamed anew as she fought for life, for her own life, for the life that was about to begin in her, for Clear Thought. She sent death roaring in exchange for death. It was all going. She sensed the re-created city turning to dust. John's mountain was crumbling. The caverns with their sensual images were filling with dust again.

Thunder came as air moved to fill the vacuum left by destruction. She was a mother fighting for a child not yet formed. She was deadly, because she believed that she deserved a chance to know that new life that was so near formation in her.

No one fought more fiercely than Stella the Power Giver.

CHAPTER TWENTY-FOUR

Old Earth's position not far from the periphery in the plane of the Milky Way allowed views of other spiral galaxies. The disk of the galaxy was viewed edge on so that it spread itself in a white band across the night-time skies. The first U.P. planets to be settled were in the same plane and gave much the same view of the stars. From all of the inhabited planets observers saw the glow of density toward the core, where man would never be able to travel. The forces at play near the core were immense. Exploration ships had been closer to the core than the sac system in only isolated cases.

The United Planets Confederation showed on star maps as a fan-shaped area, a tiny, insignificant dot when seen in relationship to the whole. Established blink routes, etched slowly and carefully by X&A ships, linked the various planets and extended outward from the Confederation in spidery lines that grew more and more attenuated with distance. No blink routes extended to the far side of the galaxy beyond the bulging central mass. It would be a very long time before an X&A explorer or an independent prospector conquered the fearful distances involved.

No citizen of the U.P. would have recognized the

vessel that traveled the unexplored regions on the opposite side of the galaxy as the yacht *Paulus*. The ship had been expanded by multiples, her design altered. Aboard her the Far Seer One Alone was deep in contemplation. He was thinking of the woman called Long Hair. He thought of her often. He had concluded that she did, indeed, escape the destruction of the Dead Worlds and that it had been she who carved the warning, for warning it was, into the bedrock of DW-I. He did not fault her for leaving a place of infinite sadness.

From her thought spheres, One Alone knew the Long-Haired one well. She had the egotism of the others, who were now dead. If she had discovered a populated planet, she would have made herself known or felt. However, at the time of the destruction of the Dead Worlds man occupied only Old Earth and Terra II.

He tried to think as Long Hair would have thought, just having witnessed the death of all that was familiar to her. If he had seen and abetted in the destruction of twenty worlds, he would have wanted to go far, far away, to the opposite side of the galaxy or even out of the galaxy.

The *Paulus* was moving on mental power, her blink generator idle. No blinkstat had been sent winging back down the line of beacons leading back to the U.P. He had left the Dead Worlds as they were when *Paulus* first approached them, with two notable exceptions. To get the immediate attention of anyone who came into the sac he had not destroyed the oxygen atmosphere on DW-3. The breathable air where there had been only noxious gases would set scientists to thinking and would add weight to the warning of the inscription.

Mankind would have 75,000 N.Y. to ponder the developments.

One Alone was totally sane, unspoiled by possessing supreme power. As an indulgence he kept the form of a tall one. He liked to see the colors of the stars, and the beauty of his Dear Companion. Otherwise, aside from propelling the ship, he used his powers only occasionally. At regular intervals he sent out a call, "Long Hair, Long Hair. I am a friend."

She had managed to stay alive, but had she possessed the mental stability to ward off aeons of being alone?

He was sure that they could be friends. Together they would search and discover and delve into the secrets of the universe until it was time, 75,000 N.Y. into the future, to return to the sac system for the next experiment.

One Alone had great faith. He believed that everything in nature had its purpose. Nothing that had happened could change his deeply ingrained conviction that there was a supreme force and that that force represented the ultimate wisdom. Nature was unfathomable, but invariably right. Nature advanced life. Species passed into extinction but were replaced by other life-forms to fill the vacant space in the ecosystem. Intelligent races had died, but not by acts of Nature.

Therefore it was evident that Nature created the sac system for a reason, for a definite purpose. It was beyond One Alone's capacity to define that purpose, but neither could he question it. He was a man and mere man could not destroy one of Nature's most complicated creations, the sac system with its conjunctional force, without risking disruption of Nature's overall plan. He had come to the inevitable conclusion that his only choice was to allow the natural forces to operate without hindrance from him.

The exposure of intelligent life to the aurora had come too soon. Those who had been altered, both the tall ones and those from the United Planets, had not yet matured. Perhaps in 75,000 N.Y. the race might be ready for a great leap forward, might have developed the wisdom to handle the gifts of the conjunction intelligently. If not, he could wait for another 75,000 N.Y. when there would be another aurora. Now there was time for contemplation. There was time for many things. In 75,000 N.Y. he could chart the entire galaxy.

There was also plenty of time to remember and analyze the past, to remember how he had spoken a prayer from the fragmentary works of Rose the Healer over the dust of his former companions, to remember how he had seen history repeat itself. His friends, even though they were more mature than the childlike people of the Dead Worlds, had followed the same path to disaster.

Only a few times in history had a Far Seer used his power of life and death. The decision had not been an easy one. The taking of a life is the most profound of all acts. On Old Earth it had never been done without a conference of Elders, but he had been forced to take action alone.

He had no doubt that he had acted rightly, but that did not ease his pain. On the last day John had shown promise, turning back to his work, but then he had transported innocent people to see his work of art. LaConius had been contemplating dictatorship of the galaxy. Cecile had been indulging in her usual extravagances and Martha had forgotten her sworn duty to her home planet. Worst of all, Clear Thought and Stella had been interested only in sensual gratification.

"Long hair, Long Hair. I am a friend." He sent the thought message surging outward into the stars.

Yes, he had acted properly. It did bother him that there'd been no time to remove to safety the innocents, the humans who had been abducted, but their deaths had been necessary for the general good, to avert the possibility of the death of billions. He was grateful to the supreme power that he had been given the strength to do the deed slowly, slowly enough to impart to the dying his immense sorrow.

Poor Stella. Her last thought was for the life that was being joined in her. John surprised One Alone by trying to throw an umbrella of protective force over the others, not thinking of himself at all.

He wept when it was all over and, through review, he saw that Clear Thought had made no attempt to meet force with force. The Healer recognized the death message of a Far Seer and submitted while confessing his sins. His last thoughts were a plea to Nature for forgiveness.

It had not been easy. For all of his preparation he had miscalculated. They had a combined strength that made the outcome doubtful and in the struggle, in the crashing thunder of power, writhing sheets of flame and destruction ran wild to consume all of the reconstructions and to leave only rubble as history repeated itself. It had been, he thought, rather magnificent.

He would never forget them. He forgave them their excesses and indolence. He loved them.

"Long Hair, Long Hair. Come to me."

He would be alone in space for a long, long time. It was a matter of practicality, perhaps even of mental stability, to be allowed one small indulgence. He performed certain alterations in the brain and body of the comatose Keeper and spent months of that timeless existence programming blankness with knowledge and skills. Dear Companion's limbs were made shapely. She walked. Her arms, once feeble and uncoordinated, were strong. He returned himself to his own form, squat, awkward, eyeless, before he opened her awareness.

She looked at him and smiled. "My love," she said, "I have slept so long."

"Are you rested?" he asked.

"Yes," she said.

Her eyes were blue. She was so beautiful. He had not tampered with her feeling for him, although he had instilled an awareness of their past relationship in her conscious brain. He held his breath. She smiled and held out her slim, graceful arms. "I miss you when you're not near me, my love," she said. "Even when I sleep."

He expanded *Paulus* for her comfort. He made a small garden with a pool of clear water in which she swam. She was a great help to him in his habitual measuring and observing for she could tap her unconscious mind wherein was stored the science and lore of the race. Although it seemed to make no difference to her, he assumed the shape of a tall one for convenience and mobility.

"Will you tire of me before the end of 75,000 N.Y.?" she asked as he held her close.

"No," he said. "For there is infinity to explore, and much work to be done."

"And?" she asked, making suggestive motions with her hips.

"Yes," he said. "Yes, yes, yes."

CHAPTER TWENTY-FIVE

"I'm Mark Jarrman and we're back with more *Cosmos*. Our guest today is Professor Paulus of Xanthos University. Dr. Paulus, I'm sure that our audience has enjoyed your insight into the personalities of the members of the Dead World Expedition. In the brief time we have left will you please give us your opinion as to the meaning of the altered inscription on DW-I?"

"I think it's perfectly clear, Mark. The big question is not what it means, but why was the inscription altered and who did it? If we dismiss the possibility that members of the expedition did it as a prank, which I do, that leaves a couple of interesting possibilities."

"Such as?"

"Perhaps the *Paulus* expedition made an important discovery, something that made a profound impact on them."

"So you think that the members of the expedition could have been the ones who changed the inscription?"

"Not as a prank, but as a warning. I have come to believe that the *Paulus* expedition felt it necessary to leave us a message. I think that they wanted to clarify the meaning of the inscription."

"Why not leave a message in English? Why didn't they contact X&A?"

"Consider this. The original inscription has been in place longer than man has been in space. Obviously, it was intended to have a universal meaning independent of language. Perhaps whoever altered the inscription had the same intention, to leave a message not only for us, but for someone who might come after us."

"That's a chilling thought, Professor."

"This is pure speculation, of course, but suppose the Iboni expedition found significant information, something of such importance that it made them feel it necessary to clarify and reinforce the ancient warning. I felt a chill, myself, when I first saw holopictures of the new inscription, Mark, but I also felt a bit of pride, for if my ex-students were responsible for altering the message they displayed a grasp of my theories of written communication."

"Do you feel that the new inscription is more sinister, offers a greater sense of threat, than the old?"

"Actually, I think that it relieves us of one of our oldest fears. If we assume that the expedition uncovered something new pertaining to the destruction of the Dead Worlds we must also assume that their intent was to disabuse us of the premise that a race of planet killers came sweeping in from the outside vastness as in some fictional thriller. Personally, I think that the new inscription dispels once and for all the slightly romantic idea of a killer race hiding in the depths of space waiting for the proper time to return to do more damage."

"We have three minutes, Dr. Paulus."

"We have always considered the inscription on DW-1 to be a threat. The alteration makes it clear that it was intended to be a warning. As it is today the inscription tells us that we face some unknown danger. Remember that our ancestors messed up Old Earth with nuclear weapons. If we take the Cygnus manuscript to be fact and not fiction, then two intelligent races destroyed each other there. In both cases the peril was within, not without. I think the new inscription tells us that the only thing we have to fear is ourselves."

"Professor, I have a holo of the new inscription here. Can you compare it with the old one?"

"Yes, well. You can see that it is not nearly as complicated as the old one. The first new symbol is humanoid, meaning man or, by inference, any intelligent race. Then there is the eye looking inward. Next another humanoid form holding a simplified model of the galaxy in his hand. Two arrows point to alternate results. One result is devastation, the other? Hope? Utopia? I would think that the Old Earthers among the members of the expedition had a hand in the new inscription for there is a definite influence from Old Earther mind pictures."

"And the meaning, Dr. Paulus?"

"I'm sure that someone will refine it to make it sound more poetic as time goes on, but it's something like this: Look within yourselves and grow, or develop. If I may digress—from that point there are alternate possibilities. We tend to revert to Old English when we state maxims. I'll try to resist that temptation and stick to everyday language."

"Quickly, Dr. Paulus."

"Look within yourself and grow. You will gain the universe or you will find death."

"Thank you, Professor Paulus. A final word?"

"We are given a clear choice. It isn't often that great concepts can be expressed in black and white with no gray undertones. When we learn what the *Paulus* expedition discovered, we can live as masters of the universe or die in total destruction, the sort of destruction that struck the Dead Worlds."

"Personally I would have no difficulty in making my choice, Dr. Paulus. Our time is up. Thank you for making this a fascinating half hour. Until tomorrow."

CHAPTER TWENTY-SIX

"Hi, Mom. I'm back."

The voice preceded the materialization of a six-year-old boy dressed in a soft, comfortable shirt which was coming untucked from the waistband of his blue shorts.

"Hi, honey. Have a nice trip?"

"You bet. What's on?" He looked up at the domed ceiling.

"You tell me." She insisted on vocal communication. There was something human and reassuring about the sound of voices.

"Well, you're looking out past the periphery again. There are the rim stars and I guess that's the R-40 galaxy in the center."

"Very good," she said. "I'm proud of you."

"Oh, sure," he said. He turned and raced from the room. She contacted him by thought as he ran up the stairs.

"Have you forgotten something?" she asked.

"Sorry," he said, "they'll all be here."

"I should hope so, for my son's birthday."

"Mom?" He was in his room, tossing his clothing aside, drawing a bath by mental orders.

"Yes."

"What's so interesting about R-40? You're always looking at it."

"It's such a pretty example of a spiral galaxy," she sent. "Wear the blue suit, if you please."

"Okay."

"And no teasing the girls, please?"

"Ah, Mom."

"When you're finished, tell your father that the others will be here in less than an hour."

"Want me to wake up the brats?"

"Not just yet. I'll do that."

They were sleeping, the other three—a boy of almost five and the two little girls. She touched their quiescent minds softly and they began to stir, to come awake smiling. There were happy giggles as clothing moved through the air to wrap them. The baby's diaper was whisked away to extinction to be replaced by a dry one.

"May I come down by myself, Mom?" the five-year-old boy asked.

"Show me your route first," she said. She saw it in her mind and gave her approval. The boy materialized six inches above the floor and tumbled to the carpet.

"You were just a bit off," she said.

"I'm not hurt," he said.

She brought down the three-year-old girl who pointed to the domed ceiling and said, "Stars."

She replaced the display of nighttime skies with a pleasant blue. A brush at her mind announced that Cecile and LaConius were at the entry with their brood. She sent welcome. Her five-year-old ran to meet his great friend, LaConius the Fifth. A pretty six-year-old girl, the image of Cecile, came running into the room to greet Aunt Martha. Martha's six-year-old boy stood with his hands behind his back.

"Here's Sissy," Martha said, putting her hand on the shoulder of Cecile's blue-eyed, blond-haired daughter.

"Hi, Sis," the boy said.

"Don't worry," Cecile told Martha privately. "They really like each other. It'll work out."

"Thirteen years will gallop by," Martha said.

"We'll have our wedding, darling," Cecile said. "Don't fret."

Clear Thought and Stella's stairstep group of two Power Givers and Two Healers arrived to fill the room with youth. The adults ignored the babble and communicated on a private level.

"How goes it?" John asked Clear Thought as he joined them.

"The main work is finished," Clear Thought said. "It was a good decision to use cubes instead of spheres. Cubes are much easier to store and handle. We finished the catalog just last night and we can now declare the Library of New Earth to be operational." He winked at Martha. "Now all we have to do is teach the ravaging hordes—" he indicated the children, who were rushing out of the room toward the gardens, "—to use it properly."

Cecile sent to the children, "Why don't you all have a swim in the pool."

"Yeaaa," came the chorused answer. Clothing flew, fell to the grass. Martha's six-year-old and Cecile's bright-haired little girl transported swim wear for themselves. The others splashed nakedly into the water.

"If I had imagined in advance how much work it is

to populate a world I might have arranged to go off in space like One Alone," Cecile said.

"You love it and you know it," Stella said.

"Yes, God help me," Cecile said, patting her very pregnant stomach.

LaConius brought wine and glasses from the bar and guided the shimmering crystal stems into their hands. "To our old friend, One Alone?" he said with a wry smile.

"To the birthday boy," Cecile said.

"Whose turn is it?" Martha asked.

LaConius groaned.

"You're right, Cone, it's yours," John said. "I did it on Sissy's birthday."

"Don't we get to eat first?" LaConius asked.

"We'll go out to the terrace," Martha said.

From the terrace there was a view of rolling hills and the sea. Huge trees shaded the grounds. Native flowers added color. In the pool below the terrace the birthday boy, six-year-old Philip, was showing off for the girls. He lifted himself into the air and dropped like a sleek seal, came up snorting to do it again.

"That's too high, Philip," John said. The boy lowered himself before diving.

"I had to relocate the elephants again yesterday," Clear Thought said. "They like my wheat."

Martha made a clicking sound with her tongue. "You know, that still bothers me after all this time. We should have invented new names. Those pets of yours, Clear Thought, are not elephants."

LaConius shrugged. "And the tigers are not tigers and so on, but they look a lot like tigers, and those animals of Clear Thought's look like elephants. It does make it simple. Tiger is a lot easier to say than some manufactured word like zbsgue."

"Like what?" Martha asked, giggling.

"Never mind," LaConius said.

The talk was pleasant, the weather perfect. It was some time before Martha said, "Okay. Volunteers to dry the little ones and put them at the table."

The younger ones protested when they were removed from the water, but the grumbling stopped when they saw the goodies on the table.

"Philip has fallen in love with space tales," Martha told Stella. "The other night they dramatized one of old Paulus' short stories. It was quite interesting."

"I saw it," LaConius said. "It made me sit up and take notice. Did anyone besides me think it was rather perceptive of old Paulus to have his characters discover how to get into another dimension through the Dead Worlds?"

"I think he was guessing very closely," Clear Thought said.

"I'm not sure it's a good thing, reaching out to bring U.P. screen programs here," John said.

"I see no harm in it," Cecile said.

"We don't want to go bush," Stella said. "We don't want to forget our background. 75,000 years is a long time to be out of contact with your race."

"Less eight years," Clear Thought said.

"Time flies," Cecile said, with a giggle.

"Philip is asking where the cubes came from," Martha said.

"It's a difficult concept for one so young," Cecile said.

"He's not the only one who finds the concept difficult," Martha said. She laughed. "Hell, I don't even understand how we can zap across the space between galaxies and lift the contents of books and films and anything else we need. No wonder Philip doesn't understand."

"My Sissy wants to know why we can't all go and visit *Man* sometime."

"Philip," Martha said, not looking at the table, "don't you dare pull Sissy's braids."

"This is a good world," Clear Thought said. For comfort he had discarded his scales. He was a pleasant-looking man, with his Healer form altered only slightly. Cecile had reverted to her slim, small frame, distorted now by her pregnancy. She had discovered that she liked being Cecile. The others, too, had tired of being tall ones, or beautiful ones, and were more or less themselves.

"Can we drink that toast to One Alone now?" LaConius asked. "Sometimes I miss the old buzzard."

"Maybe he'll find us one day," John said.

"Or we him," Cecile said.

"He'll be in for quite a surprise," Martha said.

"He wouldn't like it here," Stella said. "He's happier out there among the stars with Dear Companion."

"Do you think he altered his Keeper to make her more appealing?" Cecile asked.

"Always thinking about sex," Martha teased.

"You bet," Cecile said, striking a pose to emphasize her protruding stomach.

"He might not have changed her," Clear Thought said. "It would be a matter of integrity with him."

"I don't think he'd remain alone for 75,000 years

when he could alter her and have a real companion," Cecile said.

"Well, I guess we'll know in 75,000 years," John said.

"Less eight," Martha said.

"He'll be there," Clear Thought said.

"As will we," LaConius said grimly.

White clouds studded the blue sky. There was a slight wind. There'd be rain before evening. John cleared his throat. "I keep remembering that last surviving Tall One, the one called Long Hair. Where was she during the last conjunction?"

"It had been 75,000 years. Maybe she just didn't care anymore," Clear Thought said.

"I wonder what would have happened if she had shown up?" John persisted.

"We could have handled her," LaConius said. "We controlled One Alone."

"But two of them would have been strong," John said.

"We won because we had love," Stella said. "We had love for each other when it came right down to it. And we had love for One Alone when we decided not to erase him for having tried to kill us. We acted as a team, a single concentrated force. We will do it again if we have to. We can handle anything that comes along."

Martha shivered. The crisis of eight years past was as fresh to her as if it had happened yesterday. She took her husband's hand, for they owed everything to John, their lives, the lives of their children, this pleasant world. They owed their existence to gentle, loving, considerate John, for when each of them had struck back at One Alone he and only he had used his power to place an umbrella of protection over them as a group.

It was that small edge that allowed them to recover from their shock, to analyze what was happening, and to make the split second decision as to a course of action. They united their minds and enclosed One Alone in a cocoon of force, blunted his killing power, took their time in deciding his fate.

With the reconstructions and their own creations disintegrating from the flares of force flowing over the surface of the planet like the aurora, Clear Thought suggested a solution. One Alone would not die. He would be with his Keeper, his mind programmed by their united force to believe that he had won, that they were all dead.

"I wonder if he'd forgive us now," Martha mused.

"He would listen and judge, for he is a Far Seer," Clear Thought said.

"I think he'd accept us as a vindication of his faith in the basic goodness of humanity," Cecile said.

"I don't know," LaConius mused. "He might still see us as a threat. You know Far Seers, they're like liberals in a lot of ways. They feel that they and they alone have the capacity for caring. I think we'd better be loaded for bear when we go back in 75,000 years."

"Less eight," Clear Thought said, to general laughter.

"We'll be a force to be reckoned with by then," LaConius said. "There'll be enough of us to be Watchers, if we think it time to advance the race."

"It makes me tired to think about *that*," Cecile said, rubbing a spot where the baby had just landed a lusty kick. "Being mother of a race is trying at times."

"Which brings up the question," John said.

"Here we go again," LaConius said.

"We should be no more than one million," Clear Thought said.

"That may not be enough," John said.

"It's a manageable population," Clear Thought said, "and a sufficient number to supply Watchers."

One of the younger ones, unable to reach a bowl of pudding, tried to transport it. The bowl tipped, spilling its contents. Martha arrested the blobs of food in mid-air and returned them to the bowl.

"Training," LaConius said, rolling his eyes. "Training."

"We train them as well as we can," Clear Thought said. "And we're staking our lives on each one of them, on each new arrival."

"We're still new at this," LaConius said. "We'll get the hang of it."

"No more than one million," Clear Thought said. "Let's keep the odds as low as possible."

"It is time," Martha announced, "for Uncle LaConius to do his thing."

The young ones were gathered in the great room where they sprawled and overflowed from chairs onto the carpet.

"Uncle Cone, is this going to be the same old story?" Philip asked.

"Same old story, buster," LaConius said, "and you'd better listen."

"The great battle with One Alone," Philip said in boredom.

"What's a One Alone?" a younger one asked.

"What I am going to tell you," LaConius said, "is the story of why we're here together on our beautiful world."

"Are you going to tell us why my mom is always mooning away at the R-40 galaxy?" Philip asked.

"All right," LaConius said. "Why are we adults so fond of the R-40 galaxy?"

"Because it's the Milky Way," Sissy said. She gave Philip a look of pure triumph. He sneered at her. "My dad told me," she said.

"The good old Milky Way," LaConius said. "Our home."

"If that's our home, why don't we go there?" Sissy asked.

"Because this is our home," LaConius said, to a general groan.

"You might as well get on with the big fight with One Alone," Philip said with resignation.

"The *last* fight," LaConius said. "The *last* battle. The *last* time the powers were used against life, never to be employed in that manner again. Now it all began—"

Martha dimmed the lights. The domed ceiling glowed with the night sky as seen from Xanthos II. LaConius' voice made a pleasant drone in her ears, but her eyes were on the young ones, male and female, stairstepped in age from babyhood to six. So much depended on them.

DAW

Epic Tales of Science Fiction

James B. Johnson

☐ **A WORLD LOST**   UE2498—$4.50

Rusty was a spacer, one of the last of a dying breed. Now, returning home to find his entire solar system gone, Rusty had no choice but to turn to the hated government bureaucracy for help, only to find himself faced with a conspiracy of silence surrounding the disappearance of his world. Rusty's quest seemed totally hopeless until he stumbled upon the one secret which the government would do anything to preserve—the knowledge that humankind had at long last been contacted by an alien race. . . .

Zach Hughes

☐ **MOTHER LODE**   UE2497—$4.99

Back from space, Erin found her father dead and herself heir to a mining tug called *Mother Lode* and a set of coordinates which might open the way to unbelievable wealth—or a doom beyond any human's imagining. For what awaited at her journey's end was a mystery far older than the human race. . . .

Betty Anne Crawford

☐ **THE BUSHIDO INCIDENT**   UE2517—$4.99

In a future in which Japan economically dominates the Earth, the past and the present are constantly being "rewritten" by their paid Historians. But So Pak, son of Earth's finest Historian, seeks another path—the path of "freedom." Seeking to learn the truth about two lost mining expeditions, he launches a mission on the starship *Bushido*. But someone is determined that neither So Pak nor the *Bushido* will ever return to Earth.

Buy them at your local bookstore or use this convenient coupon for ordering.

PENGUIN USA   P.O. Box 999, Bergenfield, New Jersey 07621

Please send me the DAW BOOKS I have checked above, for which I am enclosing $_____ (please add $2.00 per order to cover postage and handling. Send check or money order (no cash or C.O.D.'s) or charge by Mastercard or Visa (with a $15.00 minimum.) Prices and numbers are subject to change without notice.

Card #_____ Exp. Date _____
Signature_____
Name_____
Address_____
City _____ State _____ Zip _____

For faster service when ordering by credit card call **1-800-253-6476**
Please allow a minimum of 4 to 6 weeks for delivery.

Kris Jensen

The Ardellans:

☐ **FREEMASTER: Book 1**   UE2404—$3.95

The Terran Union had sent Sarah Anders to Ardel to establish a trade agreement for materials vital to offworlders but of little value to the low-tech Ardellans. But other, more ruthless humans were about to stake their claim to Ardel with the aid of forbidden technology and threats of destruction. The Ardellan clans had defenses of their own, based on powers of the mind, that only a human such as Sarah could begin to understand. For she, too, had mind talents locked within her—and the FreeMasters of Ardel might just provide the key to releasing them.

☐ **MENTOR: Book 2**   UE2464—$4.50

Jeryl, Mentor of Clan Alu, sought to save the Ardellan Clans which, decimated by plague, were slowly fading away. But even as Jeryl set out on his quest, other Clans sought a different solution to their troubles, ready to call upon long-forbidden powers to drive the hated Terrans off Ardel.

☐ **HEALER: Book 3**   UE2570—$4.99

With plague sweeping the native population, Terran Dr. Sinykin Inda answers the Ardellans' plea for help, only to be thrust into a conflict between anti-Terran and pro-Terran factions. And even as he struggles to save the natives, the Terran Union's control of mining operations is challenged by an interstellar corporation ready to destroy Ardel for its own profit.

Buy them at your local bookstore or use this convenient coupon for ordering.

PENGUIN USA P.O. Box 999, Dept. #17109, Bergenfield, New Jersey 07621

Please send me the DAW BOOKS I have checked above, for which I am enclosing $_____ (please add $2.00 per order to cover postage and handling. Send check or money order (no cash or C.O.D.'s) or charge by Mastercard or Visa (with a $15.00 minimum.) Prices and numbers are subject to change without notice.

Card #_____ Exp. Date _____
Signature_____
Name_____
Address_____
City _____ State _____ Zip _____

For faster service when ordering by credit card call 1-800-253-6476

Please allow a minimum of 4 to 6 weeks for delivery.

DAW

Charles Ingrid

PATTERNS OF CHAOS

Only the Choyan could pilot faster-than-light starships—and the other Compact races would do anything to learn their secret!

☐ **RADIUS OF DOUBT: Book 1**　　　　　　UE2491—$4.99
☐ **PATH OF FIRE: Book 2**　　　　　　　　UE2522—$4.99

THE MARKED MAN SERIES

In a devastated America, can the Lord Protector of a mutating human race find a way to preserve the future of the species?

☐ **THE MARKED MAN: Book 1**　　　　　　UE2396—$3.95
☐ **THE LAST RECALL: Book 2**　　　　　　UE2460—$3.95

THE SAND WARS

He was the last Dominion Knight and he would challenge a star empire to defeat the ancient enemies of man.

☐ **SOLAR KILL: Book 1**　　　　　　　　　UE2391—$3.95
☐ **LASERTOWN BLUES: Book 2**　　　　　　UE2393—$3.95
☐ **CELESTIAL HIT LIST: Book 3**　　　　　　UE2394—$3.95
☐ **ALIEN SALUTE: Book 4**　　　　　　　　UE2329—$3.95
☐ **RETURN FIRE: Book 5**　　　　　　　　　UE2363—$3.95
☐ **CHALLENGE MET: Book 6**　　　　　　　　UE2436—$3.95

Buy them at your local bookstore or use this convenient coupon for ordering.

PENGUIN USA P.O. Box 999—Dep. #17109, Bergenfield, New Jersey 07621

Please send me the DAW BOOKS I have checked above, for which I am enclosing
$_____ (please add $2.00 per order to cover postage and handling. Send check
or money order (no cash or C.O.D.'s) or charge by Mastercard or Visa (with a
$15.00 minimum.) Prices and numbers are subject to change without notice.

Card #_____ Exp. Date _____
Signature_____
Name_____
Address_____
City _____ State _____ Zip _____

For faster service when ordering by credit card call 1-800-253-6476
Please allow a minimum of 4 to 6 weeks for delivery.